Clint saw the three men who had been holding guns to Owens's back quickly turn to look at him and Mulvernon. Their eyes went wide and he heard someone shout "Take him! Take him!" Clint didn't know who it was, but he and Mulvernon had their hands full.

From the window, Tyler started shooting at the three men. As Mulvernon fired his gun, Clint decided Owens was going to need his help. Clint threw himself to the side, and hit the floor but held on to his gun. He saw Tom Graham flip his table and all five men started to get up, drawing their guns . . .

DON'T MISS THESE
ALL-ACTION WESTERN SERIES
FROM THE BERKLEY PUBLISHING GROUP

THE GUNSMITH by J. R. Roberts
Clint Adams was a legend among lawmen, outlaws, and ladies. They called him . . . the Gunsmith.

LONGARM by Tabor Evans
The popular long-running series about Deputy U.S. Marshal Custis Long—his life, his loves, his fight for justice.

SLOCUM by Jake Logan
Today's longest-running action Western. John Slocum rides a deadly trail of hot blood and cold steel.

BUSHWHACKERS by B. J. Lanagan
An action-packed series by the creators of Longarm! The rousing adventures of the most brutal gang of cutthroats ever assembled—Quantrill's Raiders.

DIAMONDBACK by Guy Brewer
Dex Yancey is Diamondback, a Southern gentleman turned con man when his brother cheats him out of the family fortune. Ladies love him. Gamblers hate him. But nobody pulls one over on Dex . . .

WILDGUN by Jack Hanson
The blazing adventures of mountain man Will Barlow—from the creators of Longarm!

TEXAS TRACKER by Tom Calhoun
J.T. Law: the most relentless—and dangerous—manhunter in all Texas. Where sheriffs and posses fail, he's the best man to bring in the most vicious outlaws—for a price.

THE GUNSMITH

338

PLEASANT VALLEY SHOOT-OUT

J. R. ROBERTS

JOVE BOOKS, NEW YORK

THE BERKLEY PUBLISHING GROUP
Published by the Penguin Group
Penguin Group (USA) Inc.
375 Hudson Street, New York, New York 10014, USA
Penguin Group (Canada), 90 Eglinton Avenue East, Suite 700, Toronto, Ontario M4P 2Y3, Canada
(a division of Pearson Penguin Canada Inc.)
Penguin Books Ltd., 80 Strand, London WC2R 0RL, England
Penguin Group Ireland, 25 St. Stephen's Green, Dublin 2, Ireland (a division of Penguin Books Ltd.)
Penguin Group (Australia), 250 Camberwell Road, Camberwell, Victoria 3124, Australia
(a division of Pearson Australia Group Pty. Ltd.)
Penguin Books India Pvt. Ltd., 11 Community Centre, Panchsheel Park, New Delhi—110 017, India
Penguin Group (NZ), 67 Apollo Drive, Rosedale, North Shore 0632, New Zealand
(a division of Pearson New Zealand Ltd.)
Penguin Books (South Africa) (Pty.) Ltd., 24 Sturdee Avenue, Rosebank, Johannesburg 2196,
South Africa

Penguin Books Ltd., Registered Offices: 80 Strand, London WC2R 0RL, England

This is a work of fiction. Names, characters, places, and incidents either are the product of the author's imagination or are used fictitiously, and any resemblance to actual persons, living or dead, business establishments, events, or locales is entirely coincidental.

PLEASANT VALLEY SHOOT-OUT

A Jove Book / published by arrangement with the author

PRINTING HISTORY
Jove edition / February 2010

Copyright © 2010 by Robert J. Randisi.
Cover illustration by Sergio Giovine.

ISBN: 978-0-515-14755-1

JOVE®
Jove Books are published by The Berkley Publishing Group,
a division of Penguin Group (USA) Inc.,
375 Hudson Street, New York, New York 10014.
JOVE® is a registered trademark of Penguin Group (USA) Inc.
The "J" design is a trademark of Penguin Group (USA) Inc.

PRINTED IN THE UNITED STATES OF AMERICA

10 9 8 7 6 5 4 3 2 1

ONE

Clint heard the shots—or, rather, the echo of the shot. He reined Eclipse in, stood in the stirrups, and waited. Where there's one shot, there's usually more, unless it's a professional doing the shooting. If that's the case, then one shot usually does the job.

Then the second shot came.

He sat back down in his saddle and shook the reins at Eclipse. The horse took off, and Clint guided him. He thought he had the shots pinpointed, but when he heard the third he realized they were moving—the shooter, and the target.

He hoped the target was not another man. If it was, then he was unarmed, or he would have shot back. Hopefully, what he was hearing was a hunter chasing a deer.

This was Arizona—the Pleasant Valley, actually—near Apache and Yavapai counties. He was heading for the town of Prescott to see an old friend, but first he wanted to see what the shooting was about.

He heard a third shot, and then a fourth roll through the valley and then he finally saw—and heard—something. He heard it first, thought it might have been a stampede, but it didn't sound like rampaging cattle. It sounded . . . different . . . and then he saw them. A herd of woolly white beasts—sheep—and they *were* stampeding.

He reined Eclipse in and for a few moments watched as the herd of sheep ran by. Then he saw a man on foot, apparently chasing them. When he heard two more shots he realized the man wasn't chasing the sheep, he was simply running behind them—running from the man with the gun.

The shooter was on a horse and was riding the man down. He fired again, and then the man spun in the air and hit the ground. Clint realized the shooter had stampeded the herd, and then started shooting at the man. And now he'd hit him.

Clint drew his gun and fired. It didn't matter where, he just wanted to get the attention of the shooter before he could fire again. He believed the man was out of range, and while he could have drawn a bead on him with his rifle, it was quicker to draw his pistol and fire. The shot did succeed in getting the shooter's attention. The man reined in and looked over at Clint, who fired his pistol again, then holstered it and reached for his rifle. He wanted to fire a shot that would actually have some effect on the man, but he didn't want to kill him. Not until he knew what was going on. Clint didn't want the shooter to kill the man on foot, either—if he hadn't already done so—and for all he knew the shooter might have been a lawman.

Clint sighted down the barrel and fired. A bullet whizzed past the mounted man, who instinctively ducked. He tossed another look Clint's way, then holstered his gun, turned, and rode off.

Clint slid his rifle back into its scabbard, then directed Eclipse toward the fallen man.

When he reached the man he dismounted and rushed to him, but he could see that it was too late. The man— an Indian, from the look of him—had been shot through the chest and was bleeding profusely. He could try to stem the flow of blood, possibly keep the man alive for a few minutes or more, but he knew a deadly, fatal wound when he saw one. Already the man's face was gray, his lips colorless, and the blood spurting from his chest was deep, deep red.

Clint crouched over him, saw the blood coming from his mouth. The man had seconds to live.

"Who did this?" he asked. "Who shot you?"

"G-graham," the man stammered. "T-Tom Graham. Th-the sh-sheep?"

"Scattered," Clint said, "but safe. They just have to be gathered—" He stopped short when he realized he was talking to a dead man.

Clint sat back on his haunches for a moment. He took the time to eject the spent shells from his gun, feed in live ones, and then holster it again. He stood up and looked first in the direction the sheep had run, and then the direction the rider had gone. Tom Graham, the dead man had said. The name meant nothing to Clint.

The dead man was an Indian, but he was dressed in white man's clothes. From what Clint knew of Indians, he surmised that this one was Navajo. He went through the man's pockets, looking for something helpful, but found nothing.

He had no choice but to take the body with him to Prescott. There it could be identified, and the proper people notified of his death, and of what happened to the sheep.

Sheep.

In cattle country.

Somebody was definitely looking for trouble.

TWO

When Clint entered Prescott, Arizona, he was walking Eclipse, with the body of the Navajo over the saddle. He might have attracted attention riding in on his own, but this way he definitely drew the eyes of everyone on the street.

As interested as everyone was, though, no one approached him. Some did, however, begin to trail behind him. They were curious but not curious enough to ask him themselves what had happened, so they figured they'd follow along and eventually find out, anyway.

Clint had been to Prescott before, but not in a very long time. The sheriff's office was not where it had been the last time he was in town. There were many new buildings, and he figured he'd find his old friend in one of then.

Prescott, which was located in Yavapai County, had been the capital of Arizona until 1867, when the capital was moved to Tucson. But in 1877, Prescott had once again become the capital.

He kept walking until he spotted a building that had a sign on an arch above the door that read TOWN HALL. On a metal plaque next to the door it read SHERIFF'S OFFICE.

He stopped in front of the building, lopped Eclipse's reins loosely around a post. He checked to make sure the body was secure, so that it wouldn't slide off the saddle to the ground. Then he looked around at the curious onlookers before mounting the boardwalk and entering the city hall building.

Inside he found himself in a lobby. A door to his left read *County Assayer*. On the other side the door read *Sheriff's Office, Yavapai County*. Directly ahead was a stairway to the second floor, with a hallway on either side of the stairs.

He turned right, opened the door to the sheriff's office and entered.

Sheriff William "Billy" Mulvernon looked up from his desk, frowned for a moment, then brightened.

"Clint Adams!" he said, leaping to his feet. "Goddamn!"

"Hello, Billy."

The two men met halfway and shared a warm, firm handshake.

"Been a while," Mulvernon said. "What brings you to Prescott?"

"Well, originally I was just riding by and figured I'd stop in and see how you were," Clint said, "but I'm afraid my reason changed a couple of hours ago."

"Why's that?"

"Why don't you step outside with me?"

Mulvernon took the time to strap on his gun and grab his hat, then followed Clint outside.

"Who have we here?" he said as they approached Clint's horse. "Back away, people!"

The crowd moved back so Clint and Mulvernon could approach Eclipse.

"He looks like a Navajo," Clint said, as Mulvernon bent over to get a look at the man's face.

"Anybody know him?" he asked the crowd.

There was a lot of head shaking, but someone shouted out, "He looks like the Navajo who works for the Tewksburys."

"Who said that?" the sheriff asked.

"I did." A man stepped forward.

"I want all of you to disperse," Mulvernon called out. "Go on about your day. Harry, come closer."

The man who identified the Navajo stepped up.

"Clint Adams, this is Harry Skinner," Mulvernon said.

Skinner's eyes widened when he heard Clint's name.

"Harry, take a closer look."

The thin, middle-aged man leaned over, then nodded and said, "Yeah, it looks like him. He tends the sheep."

"That's right," Clint said. "There was a herd of sheep out there that had been stampeded by the man who shot him."

"Did you get a look at the man?" Mulvernon asked.

"Too far away," Clint said. "I scared him away with a few shots, but I was too late. He rode a big steeldust, but that was all I saw."

"Harry, find my deputy, and then the two of you get this body off this horse and over to the undertaker."

"Sure, Sheriff."

"Clint, you better come inside and tell me everything," Mulvernon said.

They went back into the man's office and he went around and sat behind his desk.

"You know more, don't you?" he asked.

"Yes," Clint said. "The Navajo told me the name of the man who shot him."

"Was it Graham?"

"How'd you know that?"

"The Grahams and the Tewksburys have been at it for years," Mulvernon said. "It was bound to come to bloodshed eventually. Did he say which one it was?"

"He said Tom Graham."

"Tom," Mulvernon said. He removed his hat and ran his hand through his graying hair. "Okay, well, I guess I'll have to go out and get him."

"How many deputies have you got?"

"Two, but only one in town at the moment," Mulvernon said.

"You want some help?"

"Hate to press you into service before you've even got a hotel room," Mulvernon said, "but yes."

"No problem," Clint said. "I dealt myself into this one early."

"Well," Mulvernon said, "go across to the State House Hotel and get a room. Tell them I said the town is paying for it."

"I won't argue with you there," Clint said. "Just let me know when you're ready to go."

"We'll have to go to Pleasant Valley," Mulvernon said.

"That's in Apache County, so we may have to go to Holbrook and see Sheriff Owens."

"Owens?"

"Commodore Perry Owens, if you can believe that,"
Mulvernon said. "He's a good man, though, and I think
he's been waiting, like I have, for the explosion to come."

"What's the bone of contention between the two
families?" Clint asked. "Is it more than just a feud?"

"Get yourself checked into the hotel, and have something to eat," Mulvernon said. "We can talk about it
later."

Mulvernon stood up and the two men shook hands
again.

"Thanks for taking a hand out there," the lawman
said, "but I'm sorry this is now more than just a social
call."

"I'll be here to help you for as long as you need me,
Billy," Clint said. "You can count on me."

"I know I can," Mulvernon said. "I just wish I didn't
need it."

"I'll see you later," Clint said.

He went outside, saw that the body had been removed from Eclipse. He decided to take the horse to the
livery before he checked into the State House Hotel. If
he needed to ride out to Pleasant Valley with Mulvernon
within the hour he'd ask for the loan of another horse so
that the Darley Arabian could rest.

Even though the crowd of onlookers had dispersed,
he still felt, as he walked the horse to the livery, that he
was the center of attention.

THREE

While Clint was getting Eclipse and himself situated, Sheriff Mulvernon received word from the mayor that he wanted to see him. He only had to leave his own office and walk up to the mayor's office on the second floor. He found the man looking out his window, which overlooked Main Street. Obviously, the mayor was well aware of what had happened earlier in the day.

"Who was that who brought in the Indian's body?" he asked without preamble.

"Clint Adams."

Mayor Robert Daley turned and glared at Mulvernon.

"Oh Jesus, don't tell me one side has hired the Gunsmith?" he demanded. "That's all we need!"

"No, sir. Adams is a friend of mine. He was coming to town to see me. He doesn't hire his gun out for range wars."

"That a fact?"

"Yes, sir."

Daley turned and sat down at his desk. He did not invite the sheriff to sit.

"What about hiring out to us?" the mayor asked.

"He won't hire," Mulvernon said, "but in the absence of one of my deputies he's gonna ride out to the Tewksbury place with me."

"When?"

"Tonight, or tomorrow morning. We'll have to tell them what happened to their man, their sheep."

"We know who shot the Indian?"

"Tom Graham."

"Who says?"

"Clint said the Indian told him that before he died," Mulvernon said.

"But the Indian's dead. So we only have Adams's word for that."

"His word is good enough for me."

"What's his interest?"

"He has no interest."

"Why'd he get involved?"

"He saw a man being shot at."

"What business is that of his?"

"He saw an unarmed man on foot being shot at by a man on a horse," the lawman said. "Being ridden down and killed. Does he need a better reason to get involved?"

"What'd he do?"

"He fired at the man, tried to help the Indian."

"The Gunsmith fired and missed? Sounds like he might've missed on purpose."

"He did," Mulvernon said. "He didn't know who was who. The pursuing man could've been a lawman."

"So he scared the guy away and got to the Indian before he died, so he could get Graham's name."

"That's how it looks."

"You know the Tewksburys won't take this lying down,"
the mayor said.

"I know."

"This could finally ignite the range war we've been
waitin' for."

"I'll talk to Sheriff Owens in Holbrook about it,"
Mulvernon said. "We'll have to work together."

"Owens? That grandstander?"

"He's a good lawman."

"And the Holbrook mayor is a cheating bastard."

Mulvernon knew that the two mayors played in a
poker game together.

"What's that got to do with anything?" Mulvernon
asked. "That's between you and him. It's personal. It's
got nothing to do with the law."

"That's what you say!" Mayor Daley said. He put up
his hands. "Okay, forget that. Do what you've got to do,
but make damn sure Adams isn't working for either side."

"I know he isn't."

"Because he's your friend."

"That's right."

"That's your personal opinion?"

"That's my professional opinion."

Daley sat back in his chair. It creaked beneath his
weight. He'd put on forty pounds in the three years since
he'd turned fifty.

"Okay, talk to the Tewksburys, and bring Tom Graham in. Try to do it without starting a war."

"I won't be the one starting a war," Mulvernon said. "These people have been heading for one for months."

"Those damn sheepherders! Why would Ed Tewksbury let his family get involved with them?"

"Because the sheepherders are standing against the Grahams," Mulvernon said. "Not that Tewksbury needs another reason."

"Get it done, Sheriff," the mayor said. "And let me know when you bring Graham in. I'll talk to the judge."

"Yes, sir."

"You better be right about Adams."

Before leaving, Mulvernon said, "Don't worry, I am."

FOUR

Clint had decided to bed Eclipse down himself—to the dismay of the liveryman, who was excited to have such an animal in his barn—so by the time he got to the hotel Sheriff Mulvernon was in the lobby, waiting.

"I got you a room," he said. "It's on the side, with no access from outside."

"Good. Thanks."

"And it's on the town," Mulvernon repeated.

"You sure that's okay?"

"When I told the mayor you were here, he insisted on it, too."

"The mayor?"

"He was relieved that you hadn't hired out to either side," Mulvernon said. "The sheepherders, or the cattle-men."

"Is this going to erupt into an all-out range war?" Clint asked.

"That's what we've been afraid of for months," the

sheriff said. "Look, put your saddlebags and rifle in your room and then I'll take you for a steak. We can talk more."

"What about riding out to talk to—"

"It's over an hour to Pleasant Valley. By the time we get there and back it'll be dark. I think we should head out in the morning. Then we'll also be able to stop in Holbrook, talk to Sheriff Owens, and then go pick up Tom Graham. And maybe my other deputy'll be back by then and you won't have to ride along."

"That's okay," Clint said. "I get the feeling I'm the one who lit the match to the fuse. I'd like to see it through to the end."

"You haven't lit anything, Clint," the lawman assured him. "You just stumbled into the middle of it. Go ahead, I'll wait here. It's room eleven." Mulvernon handed him the key.

"I'll be right back."

The sheriff took Clint to a restaurant where they ordered coffee and two steak dinners. When the meals came, Clint cut the meat, found it well-done and chewy. Mulvernon told him it was the best place in Prescott.

"Which isn't saying much, I admit," the sheriff added.

Clint sipped his coffee, found it hot and strong.

"Coffee's good," he said. "Vegetables aren't bad. It's okay, Billy. Why don't you tell me about the sheep and the cattle?"

"It's been going on for months, ever since the sheep-herders arrived. Ed Tewksbury and his family aligned themselves with them as soon as the sheepherders went up against the Grahams."

"The Grahams are the cattle people."

"The Tewksburys have cattle, too, but those two families have been going at it for years. But now that there's sheep involved, bloodshed was inevitable—and now it looks like it's going to start."

"Unless you can do something."

"What can I do?" the lawman asked. "This is a blood feud that's been going on since before my time. Nothing I do is going to stop them."

"Maybe if you arrest Tom Graham . . ."

"That's what I intend to do," Mulvernon said, "but that's not going to be easy."

"Which is why you need Sheriff Owens's help."

"Right."

"And mine."

Mulvernon pointed his finger at Clint.

"As long as you're offering."

"I'm offering," Clint said, "as long as you don't want me to wear a badge."

"Deal."

Over another pot of coffee and some pie Clint asked, "What's Owens like? Is his first name really Commodore?"

"Far as I know. He grew up around Tennessee. Seems to me to be a good lawman, more than a fair hand with a gun. Keeps the peace in Holbrook, I can tell you that."

"I'm looking forward to meeting him."

"We'll go and see him first thing tomorrow. Maybe he'll want to come out and talk to the Tewskburys with us. I know he'll want in on the Graham arrest."

"How many family members have we got on each side?" Clint said.

"Damned if I know," Mulvernon said. "I don't even think they know, the families are so big. Ed Tewksbury seemed to run that family. Got William Graham on the other side, and his hotheaded brother Tom. Then there's Andy Blevins. I think he's a cousin, but I know he's another troublemaker."

"Looks like Tom may have stepped over the line."

"Oh, he's stepped over it, all right," Mulvernon said. "We're going to find out if brother Tom will let us take him without a fight."

FIVE

After the steak, Mulvernon took Clint to the Buckskin Saloon, the biggest saloon in town. It was busy, but Mulvernon's badge seemed to open up space at the bar for them. Either that, or word had already gone out about who Clint was.

They each had a beer. There were games going on all around them—poker, faro, roulette.

"In the mood to play?" Mulvernon asked.

"Actually, no."

"Not even poker?"

"Not tonight."

Several girls were working the floor, and when they came to the bar for drinks they smiled at Clint, said hello to the sheriff.

Around them the murmur of many conversations made them all incoherent, until a couple of voices began to discuss the dead Navajo loudly.

"About time somebody did somethin' about them sheepherders," one said.

"Yeah, but murder?"

"It wasn't murder," the first voice said. "It was just an Indian."

Clint put his beer down and craned his neck to see who was talking.

"Forget it," Mulvernon said. "That's the way it is, here. The town's pretty much divided in half—sheepmen, cattlemen."

"And when everything explodes, you're in the middle," Clint said.

"That's what I get paid for."

"Not enough," Clint said, picking his beer up again. "Not nearly enough."

"That why you stopped wearing a badge all those years ago?"

"That's only one of the reasons," Clint said, "but it was a big one."

"Yeah, well," Mulvernon said, "I've got too much time invested behind this tin badge to make a change now. So yeah, I'm in the middle."

Clint finished his beer and set the empty mug down on the bar.

"I better turn in," he said. "I was in the saddle a long time, and something tells me we're going to have to get an early start to get you out of the middle."

"Not a bad idea," Mulvernon said. "If I didn't have to make my rounds I'd join you."

Clint looked at him.

"You know what I mean," Mulvernon said. "See you at my office in the morning—early."

SIX

With Sheriff Mulvernon, Clint rode into Holbrook with considerably less attention and fanfare than when he rode into Prescott. Holbrook was much smaller than Prescott. There was no brick city hall to house the sheriff's office, just the more traditional small sheriff's office with a shingle out front that read SHERIFF COMMODORE PERRY OWENS.

"I'll bet he takes ribbing about that," Clint said as he and Mulvernon dismounted in front of the office. "Why not just drop the 'Commodore'? Go by Perry Owens?"

"I don't know," Mulvernon said. "I have enough trouble explaining to people how to say my last name. Let's go inside."

They entered the office without knocking. The building may have been old, but it was not in a state of disrepair, and the inside was clean, with no musty old sheriff's office/steak/coffee/sweaty prisoner smell.

The man behind the desk looked up, saw them, and

smiled. He stood, filling the room, not only with his size, but his smile.

"Billy!" he said. "Good to see you."

"I hope you think so after I tell you why we're here," Mulvernon said, shaking hands with the other lawman. Mulvernon turned to Clint. "This is Clint Adams."

"Adams," Owens said. "Well, this is a pleasure." He shook hands with Clint. "Well, what brings you both here? Sounds like bad news."

"Let's have a seat," Mulvernon said, "and we'll tell you."

"How about some coffee?" Owens asked. "I got a pot on the stove."

"Sure," Mulvernon said.

"Thanks," Clint added.

Owens poured three cups and set them on the desk. Clint tasted his, found it strong and good. Mulvernon sipped his and shuddered.

"Don't know why I said yes," he commented to the younger lawman. "Your coffee hasn't gotten any better."

"I don't know," Clint said. "I kind of like it."

"You would," Mulvernon said. "I've tasted that trail swill of yours."

"I like trail coffee," Owens said. "Haven't had it in a while. This is my substitute."

Mulvernon put his cup back down on the desk.

"Okay," he said, "this is the story."

He told Owens what happened to Clint in Pleasant Valley, with Clint filling in details here and there.

Owens looked at Clint when Mulvernon was finished.

"Is it possible you heard him wrong?" he asked. "Mebbe he said another name?"

"You mean a different Graham?" Clint asked. "Tom came out pretty clearly."

"No, maybe . . . a different Tom?"

"No," Clint said, shaking his head. "He said 'Tom Graham' pretty clearly."

"So?" Owens said, looking at Mulvernon. "We goin' out to arrest Tom Graham?"

"That was my intent," Mulvernon said, "after I go out and talk to Ed Tewksbury."

"He doesn't know yet?"

"He might know," Mulvernon said. "He probably wonders what happened to his sheep. But I haven't told him, yet. Thought you might want to come along."

"You thought right," Owens said, standing up. "Have you deputized Mr. Adams?"

"Clint," Clint said, "and no, I'm not deputized, but I'm here to help."

"We'll probably need it," Owens said. "These are two families that're just itchin' to kill each other—and there's a fair lot of them."

"So I've heard."

Owens grabbed his gun belt and strapped it on, then took his hat off a peg.

"Walk with me to the livery to get my horse?" he asked.

"Sure," Mulvernon said.

They stepped outside. Clint and Mulvernon took the reins of their horses and they all walked toward the livery. Once there, Owens went inside, saddled his horse, then walked it out.

"So," he said, "the Tewksbury place first, and then the Grahams'?"

"That's the way I figure it," Mulvernon said.

"Let's go, then," Owens said. "We've got a lot of ridin' ahead of us."

The three of them mounted up.

"When's the last time you checked your weapons?" Clint asked.

"Every day," Owens said with a smile. "Bet you do the same."

SEVEN

During the ride to the Tewksbury place they passed a herd of cattle, and later a herd of sheep.

"What's the big argument against sheep?" Clint asked the two lawmen. "I've never really been clear on that."

"The cattlemen say that when the cows graze they leave something behind," Mulvernon said, "and then the fields grow again."

"The sheep," Owens said, "graze down to the roots. They leave nothing behind. Nothing grows back."

"Well," Clint said, "that makes the cattlemen's argument sound pretty strong, doesn't it?"

"Somethin' could be worked out, though," Owens said. "It doesn't have to come to bloodshed. What good is the land if it's soaked in blood? How's that gonna nourish sheep or cattle?"

"I don't know," Clint said.

"Coming up on the Tewksbury place," Mulvernon told them. "There's going to be sentries."

"You wanna do the talkin'?" Owens asked.

"The killing took place in my county, so I guess so," Mulvernon said.

"Okay," Owens said.

"No guns unless I snake mine, okay?" Mulvernon said.

"Well, okay," Clint said, "but we could all be dead by then."

They all rode toward the Tewksbury place laughing.

By the time they came within sight of the Tewksbury house they had three sentries riding with them, holding rifle stocks pressed to their thighs, barrels pointed up. Not a word was spoken.

They rode up to the house and stopped. Ranch hands came and stood around them, and a man came out of the house and stood there, just in front of the door. He was tall, in his fifties, unarmed.

"Two sheriffs," he said. "Guess we should be honored."

"Ed," Mulvernon said.

Commodore Perry Owens stood by his word and simply nodded at Tewksbury, letting Sheriff Mulvernon do all the talking.

"Whose deputy is this?" Tewksbury asked, indicating Clint.

"No deputy," Mulvernon said. "This is a friend of mine, Clint Adams."

There was some muttering from the dozen or so men surrounding them. Some stepped back, some put their hands on their guns.

"What brings the Gunsmith out here?" Ed Tewksbury said.

"He's just riding along with me," Mulvernon said. "Ed, we've got some bad news."

"This about my Indian?"

"The Navajo's dead," Mulvernon said.

"What happened?"

"He was gunned down, and the sheep he was tending scattered."

Tewksbury looked around at his men—Clint wondered how many of them were related to him—then looked back at the three men.

"What happened?" Tewksbury asked, again. "Who killed him?"

Now everyone stood quietly, waiting. The tension in the air was palpable.

"Tom Graham," Mulvernon said.

"How do you know that?"

"Clint was a witness."

Tewksbury looked at Clint.

"From a distance," Clint said. "I was too far away to help him. I fired a few shots to scare the shooter off, but when I rode down to your man he was too far gone. I tried to make him comfortable, but he only lived long enough to tell me who shot him."

"Clint brought the Navajo into town," Mulvernon said. "The body is at the undertaker's. You can pick it up there anytime you want."

"I'm obliged to you, Mr. Adams," Ed Tewksbury said.

Clint shrugged. "I just did the decent thing."

"Not too many people around today worried about

doin' the decent thing," Tewksbury said. "You have my thanks."

"You're welcome."

"I'm not gonna invite you in for a drink, Sheriff," Tewksbury said. "You understand?"

"I understand, Ed," Mulvernon said. "Now you understand something. We're riding over to the Graham place to arrest Tom. I don't expect to see you, or any of your family or men there."

"You won't, Sheriff," Tewksbury said. "You won't see any of us. I guarantee it."

EIGHT

The sentries accompanied Clint, Mulvernon, and Owens for about a mile after they left the Tewksbury house, then veered off and left them. The three of them remained silent the whole time.

"Well," Clint said, "that went well."

"Mebbe," Owens said.

"What do you mean?" Clint asked.

"I didn't like the way Tewksbury said we wouldn't see him or any of his people."

"You think he meant we wouldn't see him . . . doing whatever they're going to do?"

"That's what I think," Owens said.

"Me, too," Mulvernon said. "We better get to the Graham place fast."

They all gigged their horses into a run.

* * *

They ran into the same situation as they approached the
Graham place. Guards approached them, weapons ready
until they saw the two badges.

"We need to see William Graham," Mulvernon said.

"Follow us," one of the two guards said.

They followed them all the way to the Graham
house, which was larger than the Tewksburys'. Once
again they were virtually surrounded by ranch hands
while they waited for the Grahams to make their ap-
pearance. When the front door of the house opened only
one man stepped out.

"William," Mulvernon said.

"Sheriff," Graham said. He looked at Owens. "Sheriff." Then he looked at Clint. "Adams."

The Grahams obviously had a better idea of what was
going on in town than the Tewksburys did—which wasn't
particularly good.

"You know who I am?"

"Of course," Graham said. "I knew as soon as you
rode into town."

"Then you know why we're here," Mulvernon said.

Graham looked at the lawman. "You're lookin' for my
brother, Tom."

"Right."

"He's not here."

"William—"

"Come inside and have a look," Graham invited. "He's
not here."

"Where is he?"

"I don't know—and before you say anything, let me
explain." Graham was roughly the same age as Ed Tewks-

bury. Clint wondered how much younger Tom Graham was?

"You know what Tom did, William," Mulvernon said.

"I know, and I didn't okay it. So when Tom came back here I made him leave. I told him he couldn't stay here."

"So where did you send him?"

"I only sent him away," Graham said. "I didn't tell him where to go."

"You did that so you couldn't tell us where he is if you wanted to, right?" Owens asked.

"That's right."

Apparently, Owens felt freer to speak here because the Grahams lived in Apache County, while the Tewksburys lived in Yavapai County.

"I wouldn't give up my brother," Graham said, "but now I can't."

"He killed a man, William."

"He killed an Indian," Graham said, "and an Indian that worked for Tewksbury." He shrugged, as if neither of those things mattered.

"He still killed a man," Owens said, "and he has to pay the price."

"Go and find him, then," Graham said, "but you won't get any help here."

"What about what he did?" Mulvernon pressed.

"What about it?"

"Does anybody else here intend to do the same thing?" Mulvernon asked.

"I don't know," Graham said. "I can't speak for everybody. I can only tell you I didn't give my okay to Tom."

"And does everybody here need your okay to act?" Clint asked.

"Yes," Graham said, "they do."

Owens and Mulvernon exchanged a glance.

"Why doesn't that make me feel any better?" Commodore Owens asked.

"I know just how you feel," Mulvernon said.

"Is that all?" Graham asked.

Clint wondered if they should take Graham up on his offer to look in the house, but before he could say anything, Sheriff Mulvernon said, "I guess that's it." He looked at Owens. "Unless you can think of something else, Sheriff?"

"Not right now, Sheriff."

"Clint?"

"Well," Clint said, "we could go inside the house and have a look."

The men around them stirred.

"Yeah, you could do that," Graham said, "but I'm no liar."

"I have to agree," Owens said. "I've never known William to lie."

Kill, Clint thought, but not lie. Well, yeah, he'd known men like that, himself. Men with their own peculiar brand of honor.

"Okay, then," he said.

"We'll be looking for Tom, William," Owens said. "When we find him we're gonna put him on trial."

"You'll try," Graham said.

"And I'd watch out for the Tewksburys," Mulvernon added. "They might try to, uh . . ."

"Yeah," William said, "they'll try, too."

NINE

This time when they rode away from the house they had no company.

"You're sure about him telling the truth?" Clint asked, as they reined in when they were far enough from the house.

"He always has, up to now," Owens said. "Seems to be somethin' he takes real serious."

"His brother's wanted for murder, though," Clint said.

"You want to go back and take a look?" Owens asked.

"Even if he was in the house, he's gone now," Mulvernon said, "but I'm with you, Sheriff. I think Graham was telling the truth. He sent his brother away so he wouldn't know where he was."

"So what do we do now?" Clint asked.

"We look for him," Mulvernon said. "By that, I mean Sheriff Owens and me. Him in Apache County, and me in my county."

"I might as well ride back to Holbrook, and you to

Prescott," Owens said. "I'll mount a search from my end, and you from yours."

"Right."

Owens looked at Clint.

"Your mayor know you was comin'?"

"Yes," Mulvernon said. "You going to tell yours?"

"I dunno," Owens said. "Only if I have to."

"Your mayors don't get along?" Clint asked.

"They play poker together," Mulvernon said.

"They each think the other one cheats," Owens said.

"Then why continue to play?" Clint wondered.

"It's what they do," Owens said.

"I've got the weirdest feeling they really like each other," Mulvernon said.

"Odd relationship," Clint commented.

Owens looked at him. "Are you gonna hang around?"

"Sure, why not?" Clint asked. "Might as well see it through."

"Come back to Holbrook sometime," Owens said. "We got better steaks."

"That's not saying much" Mulvernon laughed. "That invite include me?"

"Why not?" Owens said, shaking hands with both men. "I'll be talkin' to ya."

"Sheriff," Mulvernon said.

Owens rode off toward Holbrook. Clint and Mulvernon turned their horses in the direction of Prescott.

"He seems competent," Clint said. "Stayed calm the whole time, even when we were surrounded."

"He's good under pressure."

They rode awhile in silence and then Clint asked, "You got any ideas about where to look for Tom Graham?"

"One or two," Mulvernon said. "The Grahams have friends in both Prescott and Holbrook. I'll bring some of them in so I can question them. Meanwhile, I can send my deputies out to a couple of places he might hide out."

"And what do you think the two factions will do?" Clint asked.

"The Tewksburys will probably go after the Grahams," Mulvernon said. "They'll look for Tom first, but if they can't find him they're likely to go after any Graham, or anyone working for them."

"And if that happens?"

"If that happens," Mulvernon said, "I'm going to have a full-scale range war on my hands."

"That happens," Clint said, "you'll probably see some fresh guns coming in."

"Oh yeah," Mulvernon said, "I really needed to hear that."

TEN

Back in Prescott, Clint and Sheriff Mulvernon put their horses in the livery and then went back to the same restaurant for a meal. This time Clint stayed away from the steak. He ordered beef stew. Mulvernon stayed with the steak.

"It's a habit," he said with a shrug.

"What happens when we go to Holbrook and have a better one?" Clint asked.

"Then I probably won't be able to eat steak here again."

They had beer with supper instead of coffee. While they sat there and ate, it got dark outside.

"I'll get my deputies together in the morning and have them ride out to do a search. Sure glad the second just returned" the lawman said. "There are two places he might hide that I know of. If he's not there, then maybe we'll get something from his friends."

"If we can find him before the Tewksburys try for their revenge, we might keep the lid on the range war."

"Yeah," Mulvernon said, "maybe."

Like the night before, they walked over to the saloon and took a spot at the bar. This time, however, Mulvernon's two deputies came in to join them.

"Clint, this is Jake and this is Tyler," Mulvernon said. "Boys, meet Clint Adams."

The two young deputies looked suitably impressed.

"A real pleasure, Mr. Adams," Jake said.

"Never thought I'd get to meet the Gunsmith," Tyler said.

"Just call me Clint."

"Sheriff never tol' us he knowed ya," Tyler said.

"There's a lot I've never told you two," Mulvernon said. "But I've got a lot to tell you right now."

He told them about the two meetings they had that day, and what they were going to have to do the next day.

"You know the two places I'm talking about?" he asked them.

"Sure, Sheriff," Tyler said. "We know where they are."

"We'll split up and cover both—" Jake started, but the sheriff cut them off.

"No, I don't want you splitting up," he said. "Stay together."

"Is there gonna be somebody with Tom Graham, Sheriff?" Jake asked.

"Probably not, but I don't want to take any chances. Stay together, you hear?"

"Yeah, Sheriff, we hear," Tyler said.

"Go do your rounds, then," Mulvernon said. "After that you can come in and have one beer each."

"Yessir," Jake said. The two deputies went back outside.

"What the hell are ya doin', Sheriff?" somebody said.

Clint and Mulvernon turned to find a group of five men facing them. They all looked like they'd just come in off the range, dust and dirt left plastered to their skin when the sweat had dried. And they'd all had a few drinks, to boot.

"What are you talking about, Charley?" Mulvernon asked the spokesman.

"We hear yer lookin' for Tom Graham."

"That's right," Mulvernon said, "and I was going to ask you boys if you had any idea where he might be hiding out."

"We wouldn't tell ya if we did know," Charley said, "would we, boys?"

"Well, you would if I tossed you into a cell," Mulvernon said.

"You can't do that," Charley said. "We ain't done nothin'. You can't throw us in jail if we ain't done nothin'."

"We'll see about that tomorrow," Mulvernon said. "That's when I'm going to come to you five with the question. One of you better have an answer, or I'll toss the lot of you in jail for obstructing justice."

"There ain't no such law," Charley said. He looked at his friends and asked, "Is there?"

Then he looked at Clint.

"Yes," he said, "there is."

"That ain't fair!" Charley said. "All Tom did was kill an Indian."

"The Indian Wars have been over a long time, Charley," Mulvernon said. "Didn't you hear?"

The five men, who had been spoiling for a fight, were confused.

"You boys better get home," Mulvernon said.

"We got drinks comin'," Charley said.

Mulvernon looked at the bartender.

"No more drinks for them, you hear? Or I'll throw you into a cell."

"Yessir."

Mulvernon looked back at the five men.

"That's it, you boys are done."

They looked like they wanted to protest, but Clint moved up and stood right next to Mulvernon, and together they stared the five men down.

"Damn it!" Charley said. "Let's go, boys."

Charley stormed through the batwing doors, but the other four just sort of drifted after him, not sure what had just happened.

"Thanks for standing with me," Mulvernon said, "but those five never would have pushed it. They were just drunk."

"Looks like you know your people," Clint said, moving back up to the bar and grabbing his beer.

"Knowing them keeps me from shooting any of them unnecessarily."

Clint turned with his beer in hand and leaned back against the bar.

"Gonna do some gambling tonight?" Mulvernon asked.

"I was thinking about it," Clint said. "We don't have an early day tomorrow, do we?"

"You don't," the lawman said. "I have to go and see the mayor, tell him what happened. He's real concerned about this turning into a war."

"Well, I think I'll play some poker, then," Clint said. "Whenever you need me tomorrow, just find me."

"Good luck."

Clint finished his beer, set the empty mug down, and went to check out the tables.

ELEVEN

Clint woke the next morning with a warm butt pressed up against his. He'd awakened this way many times before, sometimes a warm hip, sometimes a thigh, or a pair of breasts pressed into his back. It was never unpleasant. But on occasion it was confusing, because he didn't always remember who it was or how she got there.

This was one of those times.

He thought back to the night before. He'd spent it in the saloon playing cards? A saloon girl? Not if he'd had to pay her. But where else would he have met a woman—and then it came to him.

Poker.

He had checked out three poker games that were going on, but from his position at the bar he hadn't seen that one of the players was a woman.

A beautiful woman, who seemed to be taking all the money at her table.

Once he sat down and started to play he cut into her

profits, but she didn't seem to mind. She was throwing
him hot looks across the table, and pretty soon they forgot about the other players who came in and out of the
game as either Clint or the lady busted them.

The lady . . . He couldn't just call her that. He'd introduced himself to all the players as he sat down, and
they had, in turn, introduced themselves. His eyes had
been on her full-lipped mouth, and her even fuller cleav-
age as she introduced herself.

What had she said her name was?

She shifted her butt against him, the smooth, warm
skin having an effect on him. As his cock hardened, it
occurred to him that women didn't like it when you forgot their names, especially after a night of passion.

He lay still while she continued to shift, not waking,
only nestling herself even more tightly against him with
a contented sigh.

Good, he had more time to dredge up her name from
the muddy depths of his memory.

Why couldn't he remember? He knew he hadn't been
drunk last night, because he didn't drink when he played
poker. He'd only had that one beer with the sheriff.

He remembered when the two deputies had come
back in for their one beer each, remembered when all
three lawmen left the saloon.

And then what?

And then lots of poker and hot glances.

He recalled that when the table got down to just the
two of them, it was late, and they decided there was something else they'd rather do. They discovered they were both
staying in the hotel, so they had come up to his room . . .

Wait. His room?

He looked around. He was sure the hotel rooms were identical, but yes, there were his rifle and saddlebags, so this was his room, his bed. . . .

They'd come up here and he had taken his sweet time disrobing her, slowly bringing her flesh into view. He kissed every inch of her, finding the skin soft and warm on his lips. She sighed as he peeled the fabric from her breasts and kissed the flesh around her nipples before devoting himself to the dark brown, rather large nubs. As he chewed them she gasped and held his head in place. She was a tall, lean woman with long legs, a small bottom, not much of a waist, but by God, those breasts just stood out from the rest of her—"stood out" in more than one way.

He held their weight in his hands and continued to suckle her nipples for several minutes before he went back to disrobing, taking off the rest of her clothes until she stood totally naked.

Had he said her name at that point? He must have. He remembered her body, oh he remembered that very well. He could see in his mind's eyes the size and shape of her breasts and nipples, he remembered kissing her long graceful neck, remembered sliding his hand down between her legs, finding her sticky wet. He recalled anxiously moving down her body until his face was nestled, his tongue poking through the forest of her black pubic hair until her fragrant wetness covered his cheeks.

He could bring all of that back, so why couldn't be unearth her name?

He remembered her saying his name, "Clint, Clint," as he continued to lick and suck her, as her legs and belly began to tremble, and then shouting it as she was pushed over the edge . . .

He must have said her name when she took her turn, when she drew the length of his swollen cock into her mouth and began to wetly, avidly suck him. He knew he shouted when he exploded into her mouth, as she sucked him to completion, then mounted him and stuffed his still hard cock inside her, rode him to yet another explosion, one that was as painful as it was pleasurable . . .

She moved again, this time breaking the contact between them. She was waking up. *Come on, come on, what's her name* . . .

She stretched and he rolled over so he could watch her big breasts flatten out against her ribcage. Her nipples were already hard, and so was he.

She looked at him and smiled, then looked down and smiled even wider.

"You always wake up like that?"

"Do you always wake up like *that*?" he asked.

She wasn't sure what he meant but then realized what he was looking at, and had the good grace to blush.

"I'm afraid I do," she said, "but feel how wet I am."

She took his hand and placed it between her legs, found her wet and hot.

"I don't always wake up like that," she said, rubbing his hand over her. She closed her eyes and moaned as he took over, slid two fingers inside her, and slid them in and out.

"Oooh," she said.

Okay, he thought, this would keep him from having to say her name, yet.

TWELVE

He rolled on top of her and wasted no time poking his cock into her sopping pussy. She gasped, wrapped her slender but strong legs around him and urged him on as he fucked her hard and fast. He meant to go slower to give him time to think, but once he was inside her steamy depths he couldn't help himself.

"Oh, yeah, baby," she gasped, "like that, uh-huh, harder, harder, good, good . . ."

He felt her shudder and climax several times before he clenched, tried to hold back, and failed because it was too good to stop. He let loose inside her, and she shouted and tightened her thighs around him, using her cunt to suck every last drop from him . . .

"Oh God!" she said, moments later, lying on her back. Her body was dappled with sweat, the sheen making her breasts look as hard as rain-soaked boulders.

And then it came to him in a flash, the name he'd been looking for all this time.

"That was a hell of a way to wake up," he said to her, "but how about some breakfast, Lady Grace?"

That's what she had told everyone her name was, "Lady Grace."

Maybe at breakfast he'd get the story behind that.

Sheriff Mulvernon presented himself very early at the mayor's office. In fact, he was there waiting when the mayor walked in. The man stopped short and stared at him in surprise.

"Didn't you have breakfast?"

"I thought you'd want to hear how it went yesterday, so I came here first."

"Hmph, well, I had breakfast with my wife." The mayor walked around behind his desk. "You should get yourself a wife, Billy. Do you a world of good."

"Don't think my job would let me give a woman enough attention," Mulvernon said. "You want to hear what happened?"

"Of course I do, man," the mayor said. "Sit down and start talking."

"Did you see that bastard mayor in Holbrook?" Mayor Daley asked when Mulvernon was finished.

That was all he could think about.

"No," the sheriff said. "I left it to Sheriff Owens to talk to his mayor. I came back to talk to you."

"So what are you going to do now?"

"I'm going to try to find Tom Graham before anybody else gets killed."

"Do you think you can?"

"Frankly? No."

"Then what—"

"I think we're going to have a full-scale range war on our hands."

"Jesus—and this is an election year."

"Yeah, well, you'll not only lose some votes, you're going to lose some voters."

"That's not funny, Sheriff!"

"It wasn't meant to be . . . sir."

At the breakfast table that morning Ed Tewksbury said, "Will, I want you to go out and get the horses saddled."

"By myself?" William Jacobs asked.

"No, stupid," John Tewksbury said, "get some of the men to help you."

"Okay," the young man said.

"Do it now," Ed said.

"I ain't finished eatin'!" Jacobs complained.

"Yeah, you have," John said. "Go and do it!"

Grumbling, Jacobs got up and went out.

"What are we gonna do?" John Tewksbury asked. The other six men looked at Ed Tewksbury for the answer to that question.

"We're goin' to the Graham place," Ed said. "We're gonna kill Tom Graham."

"And if Tom ain't there?"

"We'll kill whoever is," Ed said, "and then we'll keep lookin' for Tom."

"I don't know why we got involved with these sheep people in the first place, Ed."

"That was my decision, John," Ed said. "When I die and you're the older brother, then you can make all the decisions."

"I ain't lookin' forward to that," John said.

"We ain't, either," younger brother Lane said from across the table.

"Shut up," John said.

"All of you shut up," Ed said. "Check your weapons, I don't want anybody's gun misfiring today. Got it?"

All the family members at the table nodded.

THIRTEEN

"I made it up."

"What?" Clint asked.

"I made the name up," she said. "Oh, my name is Grace, but I made up the 'Lady' part."

"Why?"

She shrugged.

"It just sounds better," she said. "You know, like 'Poker Alice'?"

"Have you ever played with Poker Alice?"

"Oh, no," Grace said. "I've never played with anybody of that caliber—I mean, until you sat down at the table last night."

"Me?"

"Well, come on, Clint," she said. "You played with Alice, right?"

"Yes, once."

"And Bat Masterson? Luke Short? Ben Thompson?" she said.

"Well, yes—"

"I'd give anything to play in a game with those people."

"Why haven't you?"

"I'm not that good," she said.

"You seemed to be pretty good last night."

"Oh, I can take money from a bunch of town farmers in a small town, but you saw what happened as soon as you sat down."

"You won last night," he reminded her.

"Yeah, but I was way ahead until you sat down," she said. "You cut into my profits by a wide margin."

"Sorry."

"Don't be," she said. "I learned a lot from you in just the short time we played." She giggled. "And then again last night."

"I learned a lot from you, too."

"Oh yeah," she said, "I'm a big expert. I'm small-time, Clint, that's why I had to come up with a name like that. I never get invited to any big games."

"Well, you should," he said. "You'd hold your own against any of them."

"You really think so?"

"I do."

"Then would you introduce me?"

"What?"

"To some of the major players," she said. "Would you get me invited into some games?"

"Grace, I could but—"

She waved her hands at him, causing him to stop short.

"Never mind," she said. "I shouldn't have asked. I don't want you to think I only slept with you so you'd get me into some big games. I should earn my way in."

"Grace, you can go to Denver, or San Francisco. Either place, I can give you an introduction to somebody. It won't guarantee you a seat at a big game, but it'll give you a chance to earn your way in."

She reached across the table and grabbed his hand.

"That's all I could ask, Clint," she said. "Thank you. Should I keep the name 'Lady Grace'?"

"Why not?" he asked. "It worked for Poker Alice, didn't it?"

The waitress came with their breakfasts and they both dug into steak and eggs. They were eating in the hotel dining room, so the steak was better than he'd had the night before last.

"How much longer do you expect to be in town?" she asked.

"I don't know," Clint said. "I've gotten myself involved in some local matters."

"Like what?"

"I'm friends with the sheriff," he said. "In fact, I was only stopping here to say hello to him, but it looks like a range war is brewing."

"Range war? I've heard some talk about sheepherders, but—"

"That's it," he said. "Sheepmen versus cattlemen."

"Why does everyone hate sheep so much?" she asked.

He told her what he had just learned about sheep grazing until the land was barren.

"That makes a difference, then . . . I guess," she said. "Doesn't it?"

"To some people, yes," hc said. "In fact, I'm having second thoughts, but there must be a way to solve it without a war."

"Can you think of one?"

"Not offhand."

"Will you be playing poker tonight?" she asked, changing the subject.

"I'm not sure," he said. "I have to be available for the sheriff."

"Well, if you come in could you do me a favor?" she asked.

"What's that?"

She smiled to take away the sting and said, "Could you play at another table?"

FOURTEEN

Clint was walking toward the sheriff's office alone when he saw Sheriff Mulvernon coming from the other direction.

"Where are you going?" he asked. "Or coming from?"

"The mayor's office," Mulvernon said.

"How'd that go?"

"Don't ask," Mulvernon said. "I've got to get some breakfast."

"Your deputies on their way?"

"I got them off before I went to see the mayor."

Mulvernon looked tense to Clint.

"I've got a bad feeling, Clint," he said, explaining it. "I don't think Ed Tewksbury is going to wait very long before retaliating."

"Once he does, it won't stop," Clint said. "They'll just go back and forth until they're all dead."

"And innocent people along with them," Mulvernon said. "You eat?"

"Just now," Clint said, with a nod. "But I'll have some coffee with you."

"Let's go."

It became apparent that Mulvernon ate in the same restaurant out of habit. He ordered steak and eggs, and Clint could see that the steak was chewy, as it had been at supper. He made a note to have all his meals in his hotel.

"Why not bring Ed Tewksbury in?" Clint asked.

"On what charge?"

"What does it matter?" Clint asked. "He makes the decisions, right?"

"Right."

"So with him in a cell for a while no decisions get made," Clint said. "At least that would give you more time to find Tom Graham."

Mulvernon chewed and listened, nodding his head.

"It makes sense," he said, "but the judge might cut him free. I'd have to clear this with him."

"Not the mayor?"

"The less contact I have with the mayor the better," Mulvernon said. "He and I are going to come to blows soon."

"Why not move on?"

"I've already decided this is my last job," Mulvernon said. "I want to finish out my time as a lawman here."

"So how do you get rid of the mayor?"

"I may not have to," the lawman said. "This is an election year."

"Is there anybody to run against him?"

"Shit, I hope so."

"Maybe a range war would be enough to get him out," Clint said.

"Maybe," Mulvernon said, "but I'd rather do it some other way."

Clint poured himself some more coffee. It was the only thing the restaurant seemed to do right.

"How'd you do at the tables last night?" Mulvernon asked.

It took Clint a moment to realize the man meant at the poker game.

"I did okay," he said, with a shrug. "Your towns-people aren't very good poker players. Ranch hands aren't much better."

"And . . . Lady Grace?" Mulvernon asked him with a smirk.

"She has some talent."

Sheriff Mulvernon's smirk widened into a full-fledged leer.

"I bet."

FIFTEEN

Ed Tewksbury raised his hand, calling his riders to a halt. They were within sight of the Graham place.

"John, circle around. Somebody's gotta take out the guards."

John Tewksbury pointed to three men and took them with him.

"We'll wait here," Ed said to the rest.

"Think they're gonna be expectin' us?" Lane Tewksbury asked.

"Maybe," Ed said, "but maybe not this soon. Or maybe they think we'll go out lookin' for Tom."

"You don't really expect to find him there, do you?" Will Jacobs asked. "You just want to ride in and kill as many as we can."

"That's the plan," Ed said. "You got any objections?"

"Nope," Jacobs said. "I just wanted to get it straight in my head."

In fact," Ed said, "if Tom ain't there, I'm gonna make

sure I gun Will Graham down. I really don't care about anybody else. Killin' Will is the statement I wanna make."

He turned as a rider approached and said the two guards had been taken care of.

"It's time."

The Tewksburys rode into the Graham ranch, guns out. The ranch hands who were working were caught flat-footed with their guns in the bunkhouse. The few men who did have guns were outnumbered, and killed.

Ed had more than a dozen men with him. Many of the Graham men were out on the range. Once they were in control, Tewksbury called for Tom Graham to come out.

The front door opened and Will Graham stepped out.

"Tom ain't here, Tewksbury," he yelled. "Go look for him someplace else."

"If your brother ain't here I'll just have to settle with you, Graham."

"For what? An Indian? Or for some scattered sheep? What the hell are you really doin' here, Ed?"

"I'm here for you, Will."

Graham was wearing his gun, but he knew he was hopelessly outnumbered.

"Why don't I come down there, Ed," he said, "and we can do this man-to-man?"

"Will," Tewksbury said, "why don't you just die where you're standin' now?"

"Ed—" Graham started, but Tewksbury drew his gun and fired three times. All three shots struck Will Graham, and he tumbled down the stairs to lie in the dirt.

Tewksbury looked around at the Graham men.

"Make sure you tell Tom Graham what you saw here today," he said. "Tell Tom I'm waitin' for him."

As Tewksbury turned to ride away, his men covered his back. When he was gone they turned and rode in his wake.

The Graham men ran to their boss, leaned over him, but he was dead.

"Anybody know where Tom is?" one of them asked.

They all said no, or just shook their heads.

"How are we supposed to tell him what happened, then?" he asked. "We'll have to wait for the others to come back. Maybe one of them knows."

"What do we do in the meantime?" somebody asked.

They all looked at one another helplessly. Their foreman was out with the other men.

"Somebody better ride for the sheriff."

SIXTEEN

Mulvernon and Clint rode up to the Graham house. William Graham's body was still lying in front, with his men around him. The hands who were out on the range had not returned and would not return until later.

Clint had been coming out of the restaurant with Mulvernon when a rider came in from the Graham place with the news, so he decided to ride out with the lawman.

As they dismounted and looked down at Graham, Mulvernon said, "This is just what we were afraid of." He looked at the men around him. "Who did it?"

"Ed Tewksbury," someone said. "He rode in here with twelve men, shot up the place, killed two of our men."

"And then?"

"The boss came out to talk and Tewksbury just gunned 'im."

"Did he have anything to say for himself?" Mulvernon asked.

"Said he was goin' after Tom, next."

"Where's the foreman?"

"Out with the hands."

"Okay," Mulvernon said, "you better get a buckboard, take all three bodies into town to the undertaker's office."

"Yessir."

The men began to move, collecting the bodies and taking them to the barn.

"Jesus," Mulvernon said, "they had to be told what to do?"

"That's how they live," Clint said, "being told what to do by their boss or their foreman—and neither one was here to tell them."

Mulvernon shook his head.

"Now we have to look for Tom Graham and Ed Tewksbury," the lawman said.

"Didn't you say you had to talk to the judge in town?" Clint asked.

"Yeah," Mulvernon said, "we better ride back with the buckboard and I'll do that."

Mulvernon left instructions for the foreman to come and see him when he got back. "Also, John Graham, if he's around."

"He's never around," somebody said.

"Well," Mulvernon said, "he will be when he hears about this."

As the buckboard came out of the barn Clint and Mulvernon mounted their horses, caught up, and rode with it to town.

A couple of hours later Clint was in the saloon when Sheriff Mulvernon walked in.

"How did it go?"

"Judge Martin issued a warrant for Ed Tewksbury's arrest."

"And not Tom Graham's?"

Mulvernon signaled for a beer and shook his head.

"What's his thinking on that?" Clint asked. "Or is he just a Graham man?"

"Tewksbury shot William in front of a dozen witnesses," Mulvernon said.

"Tom shot the Navajo in front of a witness," Clint said. "Me."

"You're not from here."

"And the dead man's just an Indian, right?"

Mulvernon shrugged.

"So you're going to serve the warrant?"

"That's my job."

"Need me to go with you?"

"No," the lawman said, shaking his head. "I'll take my deputies."

"They're back?"

"Yeah."

"Find any sign of Tom?"

"Not a hair."

"Just the same," Clint said, "I'd like to come with you, watch your back. You don't mind me saying, your deputies are a little wet behind the ears."

"I don't mind you saying," Mulvernon said, "or coming along."

"What about Owens?"

"Yeah, we should go and pick him up before we go," Mulvernon said.

"Why not send him a telegram to meet us there? Or don't you have a telegraph office here?"

"We've got one," Mulvernon said, "but Holbrook doesn't. No, we'll have to go and pick him up."

"So, first thing in the morning?" Clint asked.

"Yup," Mulvernon said, "first thing."

"What are you going to do until then?"

"Right now," Mulvernon said, "all I'm going to do is have another beer."

SEVENTEEN

Mayor Daley opened the front door of his home and allowed Judge Ed Martin to enter.

"Thanks for comin', Eddie."

"You promised me a drink."

"Come this way."

Martin followed Daley to his study.

"How's your lovely wife?" he asked the mayor.

"Same as ever," Daley said, "which means she's hardly lovely."

They entered the study and the mayor closed the door behind them.

"Brandy?"

"If you don't have anything stronger."

"Brandy will do." The mayor did not want the judge to get drunk. Not yet, anyway.

He poured two snifters of fine brandy and handed the judge one. He had known the man for twenty years, since before one was mayor and the other was a judge.

Once they were both just young lawyers, but it soon became evident which of them was going to go further in their careers.

"Have a seat, Eddie," the mayor said, seating himself behind a small writing desk. It had fit him perfectly when he first bought it years ago, but as he increased in size, the desk seemed to shrink, until now it seemed too dainty for him.

"Did you make out that arrest warrant as I asked you?" Daley asked.

"I did," Ed Martin said. "Gave it to the good sheriff."

"And did he ask for one for Tom Graham?"

"He did, but I didn't give him one. I told him there were not enough reliable witnesses."

"That's good. How did he take it?"

"Not well," Martin said. "He's not happy in his job, Robert."

"That's all right," Daley said. "When I'm reelected I'll be replacing him."

"What if you're not reelected?"

Daley stopped with his snifter halfway to his mouth and looked at the judge.

"What have you heard?"

"Nothing."

"Then why ask me that?" Daley said. "Up to now I haven't even heard that I'll have an opponent."

"And that is all I've heard," Martin confirmed. "I was just . . . asking."

"Well, don't ask any stupid questions without reason, Eddie," the mayor said. "Now, finish your drink and get going. I have work to do."

Rather than finish the expensive brandy Martin placed the unfinished snifter on the mayor's desk. He knew it annoyed the man when he wasted the expensive nectar. He'd often wondered after leaving the mayor's house if the man finished his drink for him.

"Good night, Mayor."

"Good night, Eddie," Daley said. "See yourself out, will you?"

Martin executed a slight bow and said, "I know the way."

He left the study and made his way to the front door, hoping he'd run into the mayor's wife along the way. Despite the disparaging remarks the man made about his own spouse, Judge Ed Martin had always found her to be a lovely lady.

Alas, he made it to the door without encountering the lady.

EIGHTEEN

Since they weren't going out to serve the warrant on Ed Tewksbury until the next day, Clint decided to play some more poker that night. As Lady Grace had requested, he sat down at a different table this time. Since they weren't playing against each other, they each proceeded to clean up, since there was no one at either table who could match their talents for poker.

The thing about bad poker players is that they never admit to themselves that they're bad.

The thing about losers is that they will always pour good money after bad trying to get their losses back.

Clint was playing at a table filled with both, and was sure that Grace was doing the same. After a while it felt like taking candy from a baby, and the money involved was not worth the time. Clint cashed out and went to the bar for another drink.

Lady Grace remained at her table longer because, unlike him, she was playing for the money.

Clint decided to wait.

It took some hours, but Lady Grace finally cleaned out everybody in her game. The saloon girls had all made advances toward Clint, but he had put them off as charmingly as he could. Lady Grace collected her money and joined him at the bar.

"Can I buy you a drink?" Clint asked.

"I'll buy you one," she said. "I think I'm the big winner."

"Okay." Clint turned to the bartender. "Two beers."

It was getting late. All the games were over, most of the customers had gone, and even the saloon girls were slowing down. The three of them were sitting together at a table, rubbing their feet. It was actually pretty erotic to Clint. If Grace hadn't been there . . .

"Hey?" she said.

"What?"

"I'm over here."

"Oh, sorry."

She bumped his hip with hers and said, "If you like we can go to your room and you can rub *my* feet."

"Sounds good to me."

"Let's finish these beers," she said, but in the end both left their mugs mostly full . . .

This time when Clint woke with a warm butt pressed to his he immediately remembered who it was.

Things had improved.

Before he could turn over, though, there was a knock

on the door. Clint grabbed his gun from his gun belt and padded naked to the door.

"Who is it?"

"Mulvernon."

He opened the door just enough for Mulvernon to be able to see Lady Grace's bare ass on the bed.

"Oops," he said," sorry, but when I said early I meant real early."

"Yeah, okay," Clint said. "Meet you downstairs."

"Want me to saddle your horse?"

"You can try," Clint said, "but you might end up losing a finger or two."

"I'll just wait in the lobby."

Clint closed the door and returned to the bed.

"I heard," Grace said.

"You might as well stay here and sleep late," Clint said, grabbing his pants.

"When will you be back?"

"No telling," he said. "Can't even guarantee it'll be today."

"Okay," she said, starting to turn over.

"Don't turn onto your back!" he said.

She stopped. "Why not?"

"It's hard enough for me to leave your bare butt," he said, running his hand over her firm, smooth globes. "If you turn over I'll never get out of here."

"You say the sweetest things," she said, and then added, "I guess."

Mulvernon was waiting in the hotel lobby.

"Sorry," he said, again, "but I want to get to Holbrook

as soon as possible, and then get out to the Tewksbury place."

"You really think Ed will be there?"

"Can't tell with Ed," Mulvernon said, as they walked to the livery. "If he actually believes that he did the right thing he might not run."

"If he does run we've got a Tewksbury and a Graham on the run," Clint said. "Are we taking your deputies with us this time?"

"No, I'm going to leave them here in case something else goes wrong."

They got to the livery and saddled their horses.

"We can make Holbrook in two hours if we push it," Mulvernon said. Then he gave Clint's horse a critical look. "Of course, if you push it you'll probably get there well before I do."

Clint looked at Mulvernon's mare and said, "Don't worry, we can travel at your pace. Two hours is a decent time."

They walked their horses outside and mounted up.

"Clint, I've got to say I'm sorry to drag you out of the warm bed for this."

"Don't worry," Clint said, "the bed will still be warm when I get back."

"But will the woman?" the lawman asked.

"I think so," Clint said. "We seem to have a lot in common."

"You mean besides poker?" Mulvernon asked.

"Yes, I mean besides poker," Clint said, although at that moment he could only think of one other thing that might be.

* * *

On the way to Holbrook they discussed how much easier things would be if the town would put in a telegraph office.

"At least that way we'd know if we were heading into something," Clint said.

"I think Owens would've sent word if something had happened on his end," Mulvernon said.

"Now that you mention it," Clint said, "why didn't the Graham ranch hands send someone to Holbrook for Sheriff Owens instead of to Prescott for you?"

Mulvernon shrugged.

"All I can think of is I've been the law around here a lot longer than Owens has," he replied. "Maybe they just didn't think of it."

When they reached Holbrook the town seemed quiet, as it had the last time. They rode up to the sheriff's office and dismounted. This time when they entered, Commodore Perry Owens had a deputy with him.

"Speak of the devil," Owens said.

"Which of us is the devil?" Mulvernon asked.

"I was just tellin' my deputy to be ready to meet the Gunsmith."

Mulvernon looked at Clint and said, "You're the devil."

"Deputy Garrett," Owens said, "meet Clint Adams."

"Mr. Adams," the deputy said, "my name's Pete."

"Just call me Clint, Peter."

The two men shook hands. Garrett was about ten years older than Mulvernon's two deputies, and seemed to have some experience.

"What brings you back so soon?" Owens asked.

"Ed Tewksbury went out to the Graham place and gunned down William Graham, as well as a couple of other men. I've got a warrant for his arrest."

"Why didn't the Grahams come here with it?" Owens asked.

"I don't know, Perry," Mulvernon said, "but I thought you'd want to be in on it."

"I appreciate it, Billy, but there's something you and Clint should know first."

"What's that?" Mulvernon asked.

"Somebody rode into town this mornin' who might've been hired," Owens said. "We just don't know which side he's workin' for."

"Anybody we know?" Clint asked.

"I don't know," Owens said. "Have you ever heard of Tom Horn?"

NINETEEN

"I know Tom," Clint said. "I've worked with him before."

"With him?" Owens asked.

"Not the same kind of work he does, exactly," Clint said. "I don't hire my gun out, but he doesn't always, either. At the time he was working as a stock detective."

"Well," Owens said, "we don't know why he's here. I was just getting together with my deputy so we could go and ask him."

"You want me to ask him?" Clint asked. "I'm not guaranteeing he'll tell me, but at least he knows me."

"I appreciate the offer, Clint," Owens said, "but this is my town, and that's my job."

"You want us to wait for you to serve the warrant?" Mulvernon asked.

Owens bit the inside of his cheek and gave the question some thought.

"Since you'll be serving the warrant in your own county, why don't you and Clint go and do that?" Owens finally said. "I think I'll go and talk to Horn, and then ride out to the Graham place and see who's there. With William dead and Tom on the run, I'd like to see who's runnin' things out there."

"Okay," Mulvernon said. "If we find Ed I'll take him in to Prescott and lock him up. If we don't find him we'll come back here and compare notes. I'll be interested to find out what happened with Horn."

"Okay, then," Owens said, "we might as well both get to doin' our jobs."

"I have an idea," Clint said, before they broke up.

"What's that?" Owens asked.

"Why don't your deputy and I switch places?" Clint asked.

"Why?"

"Well, that way when Billy goes to arrest Tewksbury you'll be represented," Clint said, "and when you go to talk to Tom Horn I'll be along and he'll know me. It might loosen Tom up, some."

Owens looked at Mulvernon.

"That's okay with me," he said.

Owens still gave it some more thought before saying, "Yeah, okay. Why not? Pete, you go with Sheriff Mulvernon."

"Yessir."

They all left the office. Mulvernon went to the livery with the deputy so the man could get his horse.

"Horn's at the hotel," Owens said.

"Lead the way, Sheriff."

"I do the talkin', right?" Owens said.

"You're the man with the badge."

TWENTY

Sheriff Commodore Perry Owens and Clint Adams entered the hotel. Immediately, Clint saw Tom Horn sitting in the dining room alone, and nudged Owens.

"That's him?" Owens asked. "Against the wall?"

"Yup."

Owens stared at Horn.

"I thought he'd be bigger."

"Works for him," Clint said. "He's a good detective, and a dead shot. Size doesn't really matter."

Clint could see Owens measuring Horn with his eyes. It was the way he used to look at men back when he was still building a reputation with a gun. And it was the way a lot of men looked at him. In fact, Owens had looked him up and down like that when they met the first time.

"Okay," Owens said finally, and stepped into the dining room. Clint followed.

Horn was in the act of eating as the two men reached

his table. He looked up, saw the badge first, then saw Clint and smiled.

"Clint Adams."

"Hello, Tom."

"Mr. Horn, I'm Sheriff Owens."

Horn pointed with a finger that was greasy from the chicken he'd been eating.

"You're the lawman with the funny first name, right?" he asked. "Admiral?"

"Commodore," Owens said. "My name is Commodore Perry Owens."

"That's an impressive moniker, Sheriff. You fellas wanna sit down and join me?"

"We want to talk to you."

"Okay, then," Horn said. "Sit. I'll get you some coffee."

Owens pulled out a chair and sat. Once he did that, Clint followed. Horn called over a waiter, got two coffee cups and another pot.

"You fellas mind if I keep eatin'?" Horn asked.

"Not at all," Owens said.

"Where's your badge, Clint?"

"No badge, Tom," Clint said. "I'm just sort of helping out."

"I see, well, what can I do for you gents?"

"I'd like to know why you're here?" Owens asked.

"I was hungry," Horn said.

"No," Owens said, "not here in the dining room, here in town."

Horn shrugged. "Seemed like a nice, quiet town."

"It is a quiet town, and I'm tryin' to keep it that way,"

Owens said. "We've got a little range war brewin' here-abouts. Maybe you've heard somethin' about it?"

Horn bit into a fried chicken breast, chewed thoughtfully, then said, "Range war? Can't say I have heard about it. What's it all about?"

"Sheep and cattle," Owens said.

"Ah," Horn said. "Yeah, I can see where that would cause some trouble."

"You hire out for that kind of trouble, don't you, Mr. Horn?"

"I think Clint can tell you I never hire out to start trouble, Sheriff."

"No, but you hire out to finish it, for one side or the other."

"Hmm," Horn said. "I never heard it put that way before."

"My question is, are you here because you've been hired," Owens asked, "and if so, which side has hired you?"

"Sheriff," Horn said, "I can safely tell you that I am working for neither side in your little range war."

"Yet?"

"Did I say yet?"

"No, but I thought—I wondered—are you here to listen to both sides and then choose an employer?"

Horn looked at Clint.

"He's persistent, ain't he?"

"He's doing his job, Tom."

Horn dropped the remnants of the breast into his plate and picked up a large leg.

"Sheriff," he said, "I don't discuss my business. If I

did, nobody would ever hire me. Can you understand that?"

"I can try," Owens said. "Try to understand my business. I'm trying to keep any more people from bein' killed."

Horn looked at Clint.

"How'd you get into this? You don't hire out."

"I just sort of . . . backed myself into it," Clint said.

Horn pointed the same greasy finger at Clint.

"That old problem of yours of not being able to mind your own business?"

Clint nodded and smiled.

"You gotta work on that, Clint."

"I thought I had."

TWENTY-ONE

"Well," Owens said, standing up angrily, "if you're not gonna cooperate, just don't get in my way."

With that the lawman stormed out. Clint had an idea it was an act, setting him up to talk to Horn in Owens's absence.

"Touchy type, ain't he?" Horn asked.

"People are being killed," Clint said.

"Over sheep?" Horn asked. "Damn fool reason to kill or be killed, if you ask me."

"We agree there."

Horn finished his chicken and pushed the plate away from him.

"Look, Clint, I can't afford to be intimidated by the law," he said. "You understand that."

"I do."

"But I'm not the law," Clint said. "I'm not trying to intimidate you."

"But you want me to answer the question he asked me," Horn said.

"It wouldn't hurt."

Horn sat back, wiped his mouth and greasy fingers with a cloth checkerboard napkin, then dropped it on the table.

"I can only tell you this," he said. "As of this moment, I don't work for nobody in this town, or in this county."

"That's cute," Clint said. "What about Prescott, or Yavapai County?"

"There, neither," Horn said. "You pass that on to your lawman friend."

"He's not my friend," Clint said. "I only met him in the last couple of days."

"Then why are you involved?"

"I do have a lawman friend, Billy Mulvernon," Clint said. "He's the sheriff over in Prescott."

Clint made brief his explanation about why he had become involved.

"I knew it," Horn said, grinning. "You shoulda just turned and kept on goin'."

"You're probably right," Clint said, "but it's too late for that, isn't it?"

"Looks like."

"So how deep are you?"

"I'm just watching Sheriff Mulvernon's back because he's got two wet-behind-the-ears deputies."

"And this fella?"

"I just thought I'd come over here with him and say hello."

"Okay, then," Horn said. "I assume you and me ain't gonna have no trouble."

"Not unless you go up against Mulvernon," Clint said. "I gave him my word I'd see this out with him."

Horn stood up, threw money on the table.

"Come on, let's walk outside together."

Clint stood and walked with Horn out the door. Owens was nowhere in sight.

"How about if I give you my word that you won't have any reason to draw your gun against me? Would that suit you?"

"That would suit me fine, Tom," Clint said. "I just don't know if it'll suit the two lawmen."

"I'm not givin' my word to them," Horn said. "I'm givin' it to you."

Horn gave Clint a little salute, then turned and walked away.

Clint found Owens in his office.

"I thought I'd give you some time alone with him," the lawman said. "Did you find out anythin'?"

"Only that he promises not to give me any reason to go against him."

"What does that mean?"

"For you and Billy? I'm not sure."

"So we don't know anythin' about why he's here," Owens said.

"No, we don't."

Sheriff Owens sat down behind his desk, looking dissatisfied.

"I wonder if Billy and Pete are doin' any better than we are?" he commented.

"He probably hasn't even gotten out there, yet," Clint said, taking a seat. "I guess we just have to wait."

"No, we don't," Owens said, standing up. "Remember? We're goin' out to the Graham place."

"You're right," Clint said, getting to his feet, "I did forget."

"I want to find out who's in charge out there, now that William is dead," Owens said. "If we know who's makin' the decisions, we might be able to predict what they're gonna do next."

TWENTY-TWO

Sheriff Mulvernon and Deputy Pete Garrett rode up to the Tewksbury house, surprised that they had not been braced by any sentries or guards. Ranch hands looked over at them as they approached, and ignored them. As the two lawmen dismounted, the front door of the house opened and a woman stepped out. She stood ramrod straight and tall, with dark hair streaked with gray. Mulvernon knew this was Ed Tewksbury's wife. A handsome woman in her fifties, she was the matriarch of the Tewksbury family.

"Mrs. Tewksbury."

"Sheriff."

"This is Deputy Garrett, from Holbrook. He represents Sheriff Owens."

"I suppose you're lookin' for my husband?"

"That's right."

"He's not here."

"May we come inside and look?"

"Look all you want, you won't find him," she said.

She allowed the two lawmen to enter her house first, and she followed. They searched the entire one-floor structure, which didn't take long. It had four rooms, but was not huge.

"He wanted to stay and face you," she said, "but I made him leave."

"Where did he go, ma'am?"

"Into the hills, which he knows very well," she said. "You'll never find him there, unless he wants you to."

"Mrs. Tewksbury, Ed committed murder. He has to pay for it."

"By whose law?"

"By everybody's law."

"No," she said, "we don't recognize your law. We have our own, and that's what we're goin' by. So you get out of here. You searched the house, you saw he ain't here. Now you get out."

"Just tell him to turn himself in, Mrs. Tewksbury," Mulvernon said. "It's the only way."

"Don't you worry, Sheriff," she said. "We know there's only one way—our way."

Mulvernon and Pete left the house, went to their horses, and mounted up.

"What now?" Garrett asked.

"Back to see what's going on with your boss and Clint."

"And what about Tewksbury?"

"He's out there, and so is Graham. We may just have to join forces and go out and hunt them both down."

* * *

When Clint and Sheriff Owens reached the Graham place they were immediately braced by a group of men with guns. Clint could see they were all ranch hands ... cowboys, not gunmen. There were no hired guns here. Not yet, anyway.

The door to the Graham house opened and a man stepped out.

"Whataya want?"

"We want to talk to ... to a Graham," Owens said.

"Yer wonderin' if any are left, ain'tcha?" the man asked.

"You're Andy Blevins, ain't ya?" Owens asked.

"That's right."

"Mr. Blevins, are you making the decisions for the Graham family now?"

"'Course not," Blevins said. "The Grahams make their own decisions."

"Have you seen Tom since he ... since he shot down the Navajo?"

"I have, but he ain't here now."

"Are there any Grahams here?"

"John's around, somewhere."

"Then we'll talk to him."

"He's probably out lookin' for his brother Tom," Blevins said.

"Where?"

"I don't know," Blevins said. "And if I did, I wouldn't tell ya."

"So John's makin' the decisions?"

"I suppose," Blevins said. "Unless Tom is."

"While he's on the run?"

Blevins shrugged.

"Yer not bein' real helpful, Blevins," Owens said.

"Sheriff," Blevins said. "I ain't tryin' ta be. Me and my brothers will stand with the Grahams against the Tewksburys, or anybody."

"How many brothers do you have, Mr. Blevins?" Clint asked.

"I got enough. I got Charles, Sam, John—"

"Another John?" Clint asked. He'd also noticed there were a lot of "Williams" or "Wills" involved, including Sheriff Mulvernon.

"It's a common name," Blevins said.

"Blevins, you tell whatever Graham you see—John, Tom, whoever—that Tom better turn himself in. Or we'll hunt him down."

"You go ahead and do that, Sheriff," Blevins said. "You hunt him down, see how much good that does ya."

Owens and Clint exchanged a glance, then turned and rode back toward Holbrook.

"What do you think?" Owens asked.

Clint told the lawman what he thought about the men he saw.

"I suppose you'd know a hired gun when you saw one," Owens said. "No offense meant . . . I just mean with your, uh, experience."

"I know what you meant," Clint said. "No offense taken. What do you know about the Blevins brothers?"

"Just that they usually throw in with the Grahams," Owens said.

"Not related?"

"Yeah, they are.

"Makes sense then."

"Yeah," Owens said, "it does that. Let's get back to town, see if Billy and Pete have come back. We're gonna have to figure out our last move."

TWENTY-THREE

Sheriff Mulvernon and Deputy Garrett got back to Holbrook before Sheriff Owens and Clint did. They got themselves something to eat at a café Garrett picked out, then went to the sheriff's office, where Garrett made a pot of coffee. They were sitting there drinking coffee when Clint and Owens walked in.

"Any luck?" Mulvernon asked.

"No," Owens said. "Tewksbury's on the run. Went into the hills."

"Maybe he'll run into Tom Graham up there," Clint said, "and they'll kill each other."

Owens poured out some coffee and handed it to Clint, then poured one for himself.

"You mind?" he said to Garrett, who was sitting behind the desk.

"Oh, sorry, Sheriff."

Garrett moved and Owens sat down.

"We got two killings, and two men on the run," Owens

said. "Could be in your county, or could be in mine. What do we do?"

"Look for them, I guess," Mulvernon said.

"And what about the rest of 'em?" Garrett asked. "What if they keep shootin' each other?"

"Well then, you and Sheriff Mulvernon's deputies are gonna have to do something about it," Owens said.

"What about Tom Horn?" Mulvernon asked. "Whose side is he on?"

"Well, for now," Clint said, "he seems to be on his own side."

"That means he hasn't gotten a good offer yet," Mulvernon said. "He'll work for whoever offers him more money, the Tewksburys or the Grahams."

"Maybe we should keep either of them from makin' him an offer," Owens said.

"How do we do that?" Mulvernon asked.

"Run him out of town," Owens said.

"You want to do that?" Mulvernon asked. "Try running Tom Horn out of town, 'cause I don't."

"I'll give it a try," Owens said. "Why not you?"

"I'll tell you why not," Mulvernon said. "You're younger than me, and faster with a gun. You've got a better chance."

"Tom Horn is not going to draw down on the law," Clint said.

Mulvernon looked at him.

"Oh yeah? Then what's he going to do when Owens tries to run him out of town?"

"He'll go."

"Good," Owens said. "That's what we want."

"He'll go to Prescott."

Owens looked at Mulvernon.

"Then he'll be your problem," he said. "You'll have to run him out of Prescott."

"And then he'll go somewhere else nearby, where either family can still get in touch with him," Clint said.

"So what do we do?" Mulvernon asked.

"Just leave him alone," Clint said. "Concentrate on the families, not on Horn. That'll just distract you."

"Okay," Owens said. "Should we search together, or split up?"

"Each in our own county?" Mulvernon asked. "That sounds right."

"Wait," Garrett said. "If the deputies are stayin' behind, what about Sheriff Owens? You'll have Adams, but he'll be alone. Who's gonna watch his back?"

"Pete makes a good point," Clint said. "Billy, why don't you take one of your deputies with you, and I'll go with Owens. Then there'll be one deputy in each town."

"That works for me," Owens said.

"Sure, why not?" Mulvernon said. "Probably doesn't make much difference. This whole valley's a powder keg, and sooner or later it's going to go boom."

TWENTY-FOUR

They split into their decided-upon partnerships and searched the hills for Tom Graham and Ed Tewksbury. They stayed on the trail for days at a time, returned to town for supplies, and then went back into the hills.

Even though Clint was riding with Commodore Perry Owens in Apache County, he did take the opportunity to stop back in Prescott a time or two. Each time, he stopped in the saloon to see if Lady Grace was still fleecing the locals. She was, and went back to his room with him each of those nights . . .

"How much longer do you think this will go on?" she asked him.

"I don't know," he said. "Until we find the men we're looking for, or until they all kill each other. Why, are you ready to leave town?"

"I've given a lot of thought to what you told me about

Denver or San Francisco," she said. "I'm going to do it. I have enough of a stake to go to Denver."

"Good for you."

"I didn't want to leave without saying good-bye, though."

He turned his head and looked at her. Her hair was fanned out around her on her pillow. She looked achingly lovely.

"So this is good-bye?"

"I think so," she said. "I have to do something, Clint. I have to make a move."

"I understand."

She rolled over on top of him and kissed him, then dangled her breasts in his face so he could suck the nipples until they were hard. She moaned as she lifted her hips and took his hard cock inside her. She began to ride him, slowly at first, then faster and faster. Finally, she was almost prone on him, her butt rising and falling with such force that the room filled with the sound of flesh slapping flesh. She became so wet that the room also filled with the sound of her sopping pussy making *squish-squish* sounds as she came down on him.

He didn't mind any of the sounds. They just added to the eroticism of this, their farewell fuck . . .

In the morning they did it again—another "farewell"— before he left the hotel room to walk to the livery to collect Eclipse. Hopefully, next time he came back to town she'd be gone, or else it might be kind of awkward between them.

Sheriff Mulvernon and his deputy were still out of

town, but after saddling Eclipse, Clint decided to stop by the sheriff's office to see the deputy who had been left in town.

That's when he heard the story of what had happened out at one of the Tewksbury cabins . . .

Led by John and Tom Graham, and Andy Blevins, a dozen men surrounded one of the Tewksbury cabins and demanded that Ed Tewksbury come out. This was not the Tewksbury ranch, but an outlying cabin where some family members lived.

When a voice called out that Ed Tewksbury was not inside, the Graham faction opened fire on the cabin. The cabin was riddled with bullets, and because it was so poorly constructed it did not offer the people inside much protection from the flying chunks of hot lead.

The Grahams continued to reload and fire for hours. Finally, the door to the cabin opened and both John Tewksbury and William Jacobs made a run for their horses. The Grahams immediately adjusted their fire away from the house and onto the two fleeing men. Both of the men were riddled with bullets before they could reach their horses.

When the firing stopped, somebody from the Graham faction ran over to the bodies to investigate them, then returned to the others.

"Ain't Ed Tewksbury," he said.

"Keep firing," Tom Graham said.

They kept shooting at the cabin for another two hours before the door opened and John Tewksbury's wife came out with a shovel.

"I wanna bury my dead," she called out. "You wanna kill me for that, go ahead."

The woman walked to the two bodies with her shovel.

"That's it," John Graham said. "We're done here."

"We could kill her," Tom said. "That would really send a message."

"You wanna start killin' women and children?" his brother asked. "Indians, yeah, and sheepherders, and Tewksbury men, but not women and children. I ain't doin' that."

John got up and walked to his horse. Other men followed. Andy Blevins looked at Tom Graham. He always took his cues from Tom.

"What do we do?" he asked.

"Okay," Tom said, "okay, we're done."

He and Blevins walked after the others, mounted their horses, and rode off.

TWENTY-FIVE

Clint got back to Holbrook around the same time as Mulvernon and his deputy. They rode out to the cabin with Sheriff Owens and Deputy Garrett, but no one was there. They went inside and were amazed that the cabin was still standing. Sunlight shone through all the bullet holes in the front wall.

"Mrs. Tewksbury lived through this?" Mulvernon asked.

Clint walked around, found a heavy sofa overturned and full of lead.

"She must have hid behind this," Clint said.

"And what about the men?" Garrett asked. "Why didn't they?"

"They must've panicked and run for their horses," Owens said.

"The way I heard it, the shooters were here for hours," Garrett said.

"Poor woman must've finally had enough," Mulvernon's deputy Jake said.

They left the cabin, and found the graves that had been dug.

"Mrs. Tewksbury must be at the main house, with the rest of the family," Owens said. "Let's go there and talk to her. Maybe she saw somebody."

"I didn't see nobody," Julia Tewksbury said, shaking her head. "I kept my head down until I had enough, then I didn't care if they killed me. I got my shovel and I went outside."

"They didn't fire at you?" Owens asked.

"No."

They had not been allowed in the house, but she had come outside with Ed Tewksbury's wife to answer their questions. She stood with her thin shoulders hunched, her sister-in-law's arm around her shoulders.

"They rode away and I buried my husband and his cousin."

"And you didn't see any of the men who fired at your house?"

"No, I didn't see nobody."

"Why'd she have to see anybody?" Ed's wife, Ada, asked. "You know it was the Grahams. When Ed hears about this there's gonna be hell to pay."

"I think there already has been," Mulvernon said.

TWENTY-SIX

"Horn might've been in on it," Owens said, as they all got back to his office.

"I don't think so," Clint said.

"It's been two weeks since he got here," Owens said. "You don't think he's picked a side yet?"

Clint didn't know. Tom Horn was an odd man. Clint had no way of knowing why he'd stay in town so long if he hadn't picked a side. But he still didn't think the man would be part of a pack that fired on a cabin full of people for hours.

"You want to ask him?" Mulvernon asked Clint.

"It wouldn't be asking, it would be accusing," Clint said. "I don't want to do that. You do it."

"I'll do it," Owens said.

"Fine," Clint said. "You've been wanting to face Horn since he got here."

"I just ain't afraid to face him," Owens said.

"I'll back your play Sheriff," Garrett said.

"There ain't no play to back, Pete," Owens said. "I'm just gonna talk to the man." He stood up. "In fact, I'll go and find him right now. Are you boys heading back to Prescott tonight?"

"I figured we'd wait 'til morning," Mulvernon said.

"Suits me," Clint said. "Let's go get something to eat."

"Have a steak at Mona's," Owens said. "Better than you can get in Prescott, remember?"

"Guess I'll finally give it a try," Mulvernon said.

"Mind if I eat with ya?" Pete asked.

"Come ahead," Mulvernon said.

All four men left the sheriff's office together.

"I'll come and join ya after I talk with Horn," Owens said.

"Sure," Mulvernon said.

"Go easy with him, Sheriff," Clint added.

"I ain't gonna push him into a fight, Adams," Owens said. "I just wanna talk to him."

"I know it."

Owens turned and walked away.

"You think it's smart to let him go alone?" Mulvernon asked.

"Even if he does want to push Horn into a fight, Tom won't go for it," Clint said. "Let's go and eat."

Mona's was a pretty big restaurant, the largest in town, but as soon as Clint entered with Mulvernon and Garrett, he saw Tom Horn sitting in the back.

"Looks like Owens won't find him so quick," he said to the others.

"I could go and find him," Garrett offered.

"No," Clint said. "Let's just sit down and eat and see what happens."

A waitress showed them to a table for five when they told her they were expecting Sheriff Owens. They all ordered steak dinners, and a pitcher of beer to go along with it.

Horn had apparently finished eating. He stood up to leave and saw Clint with the two lawmen. He walked over to the table.

"Heard you been hunting in the hills for weeks," he said. "Any luck?"

"None," Clint said, "but there was some excitement while we were gone."

"I heard," Horn said. "Bunch of cowards, if you ask me. I got no use for men like that, put a woman in danger that way. Where's your other sheriff?"

"He'll be along soon," Clint said. "He's making rounds."

"Figure he might wanna talk to me," Horn said. "After all, he probably still thinks I'll choose one side or the other, right?"

"That's his job," Clint said.

"Guess he wonders why you're still in town if you ain't takin' sides," Garrett said.

Horn looked at Garrett, who tried to hold the other man's eyes but failed and looked down.

"That what you're wonderin', Deputy?" Horn asked.

"Well, uh . . ."

"Guess you never heard of somebody just lookin' for some time off, huh?" Horn looked at Clint. "See you around, Clint. Maybe buy you a drink later?"

"Sure."

Mulvernon watched Horn's back as the man walked out of Mona's.

"What do you think now?" he asked Clint.

"I don't know what he's doing here," Clint said, "but he didn't have anything to do with that shooting. I'm still sure of that."

"Okay," Mulvernon said, "if you say so." He looked at Garrett. "These steaks as good as your boss says?"

Grateful for something else to talk about, the deputy said, "You'll see. They do 'em with all these onions . . ."

When Owens came in he sheepishly sat down with them and ordered a steak.

"He was here, wasn't he?" he asked.

"Yeah," Garrett said. "How'd you know?"

"I looked everywhere else," the sheriff said.

"He knew about the shootin'," Garrett said, "but I agree with Clint, now. He wasn't involved."

"What makes you say that?"

"The way he felt about them shooting up that cabin with a woman inside."

"So he's a gentleman, huh?"

"I just don't see him shootin' at no women," Garrett said.

Owens's steak came fast, and he dug in.

"You were right about these steaks," Mulvernon said. "I'm not going to be able to eat back in Prescott. I'll have to stick to chicken. Or stew."

"Don't eat the beef stew here, then," Owens warned. "It'll put ya off steak anywhere but here."

Clint admitted the steak he just had was better than the one in Prescott, but he kept quiet because he'd had better steaks elsewhere.

The conversation stayed on food for a while, with most of the talk going between the two sheriffs. The two deputies concentrated on their food, and Clint watched the two sheriffs go at it.

"You're quiet," Mulvernon said to Clint. "Ready to give all this up?"

"I told you I'd stick to the end."

"Yeah, but who expected it to take this long?" the lawman said. "Look, Clint, I wouldn't hold it against you if you left."

"You've been lucky up to now," Clint said. "Neither of you has had to face a mob, or get in the middle of a firefight. But it's coming, believe me it's coming."

"I gotta agree with Clint there," Owens said. "Tom Graham and Ed Tewksbury are well hidden, but when they come out I think this whole thing's gonna blow."

"Then maybe we should stop chasing our tails in the hills," Mulvernon said, "and wait them out."

"Suits me," Owens said.

"Clint and me'll go back to Prescott tomorrow," Mulvernon said, "and we'll do our waiting in our own backyards."

TWENTY-SEVEN

Ed Tewksbury entered his house by the back door, and found his family waiting inside for him. His wife, his surviving family—mostly cousins, now—and the Daggs brothers, who actually owned the sheep herd that was the bone of contention.

In truth, the sheep had simply escalated a battle that had already been going on between the Tewksbury and Graham families. The Tewksburys were cattlemen as well, but had sided with the Daggs because the Daggs were battling the Grahams.

"Ed," Ada said, rushing into his arms.

"It's all right, Ada," he said.

"What're we gonna do, Ed?" Dave Daggs asked. "The Grahams could be comin' for us any minute."

"We'll just have to be ready for them, then," Ed said.

"Hasn't there been enough killin'?" Ada demanded. "Your brother is gone—"

"And that's not somethin' I'm just gonna let lie, Ada,"

Tewksbury said. "My brother is dead and I ain't gonna forget that."

"What if the law comes out here again?" Ada asked.

"Don't worry about the law," Tewksbury said. "I'm gonna take care of everything."

At the Graham home Tom showed up and was greeted by his brother John, all the Blevins boys except Andy, who was in town, and another Blevins man named Mose Roberts.

"We ain't gonna wait for the Tewksburys to come back at us," Tom said.

"So what are we gonna do?" Charley Blevins asked.

"We're gonna finish this," Tom said. "We're gonna hit them again, and this time we're gonna hit hard. We kill everybody—including the sheep."

"And what about the women?" Charley Blevins asked.

"We shoulda killed that one the other day," Tom said. "It's time to stop takin' it easy on these people."

"How we gonna kill the sheep?" Mose Roberts asked.

"We're gonna burn the whole herd," Tom said.

"Can we take some of it home for dinner?" Sam Blevins asked, laughing.

Sam Blevins was fifteen years old. Tom backhanded him and said, "Shut up while the adults are talkin'!"

Sam rubbed his cheek, threw a hurt look at Tom Graham, and a pleading look at his brothers.

"Yeah," Charley Blevins said to his brother, "shut the hell up!" He looked at Tom. "Go ahead, Tom, lay it out."

"I'm gettin' supper on the table," one of the Graham women said, and the other ladies went with her.

"Here's the way it's gonna go . . ." Tom said.

* * *

Andy Blevins was in the saloon in Holbrook, drinking too much and talking even more.

The bartender called over a gopher, a kid named Danny and said, "Go and get the deputy, or the sheriff. Hurry up!"

"Yessir."

Blevins was busy holding court at the bar, telling people how he had killed John Tewksbury and William Jacobs, shot them down like dogs.

"And that's just the beginning," he told his audience. "Just the beginning. We're tired of these sheep men, and it's time to drive them out once and for all . . . and anybody who sides with them, like them damn Tewksburys."

He actually had some people nodding and agreeing with him, and buying him drinks.

It took the kid Danny a while to find Sheriff Owens and Deputy Garrett. When he did they were coming out of Mona's with Clint Adams, Mulvernon, and his deputy, Jake.

"Hey, Sheriff," Danny said, "the bartender over at the saloon says you better come quick."

"What's goin' on?" Owens asked. "Is it somethin' Pete here could handle?"

"I could go with him," Jake offered. "Watch his back."

"I think you better come, Sheriff," Danny said. "Andy Blevins is there and he's really drunk."

"So?"

"He's talkin' about how he killed those two men," Danny said.

"Which two—"

"You know, Tewksbury and Jacobs? At that cabin?" Danny said.

Owens looked at Clint and Mulvernon and said, "Maybe things are breakin' sooner than we thought."

"Sounds like it," Mulvernon said. "Why don't we all just tag along?"

TWENTY-EIGHT

By the time Clint and the lawmen got to the saloon Andy
Blevins was gone.

"Ya just missed him, Sheriff," the bartender said. "Said
he was goin' home to have supper with his family."

"Home?"

"Well . . . what he said was he was going to the Graham house for supper."

Owens looked at Mulvernon.

"Are you thinkin' what I'm thinkin'?"

"Tom Graham?"

Owens nodded.

"Clint?" Mulvernon said.

"Sounds good to me."

Owens looked at the bartender.

"How many witnesses were there to Blevins admittin'
to shootin' those two men?"

"A lot. They was buyin' him drinks."

"You be ready to give me some names when we get back," Owens said.

"Sure thing, Sheriff."

"Let's go to my office," Owens said to Clint, Mulvernon, and the deputies. "I just happen to have an old warrant for cattle rustling with Andy Blevins's name on it. I think it's time to serve it."

They went by the office to pick up the warrant for Andy Blevins. Meanwhile, Blevins showed up at the Graham house, drunk and loud and telling people not to worry about anything because he'd set everybody in Holbrook straight.

"What do you mean, 'straight'?" Tom Graham asked.

"I tol' 'em what we did!" Blevins said. "Hey, what smells so good?" He sniffed the air, detecting supper.

"Wait, wait, Andy," Tom said, grabbing him to get his attention. "What the hell did you do? You told who?"

"Everybody!"

"Tol' them what?"

"That I killed Jacobs and Tewksbury."

"That you killed 'em, or we killed 'em?" Tom demanded. "Which is it?"

"You, me, us, what the hell's the difference?" Blevins demanded. "Now they know not to trifle with us."

"Oh shit, Andy," Tom said. He turned and shouted, "John!"

Andy's half brother, John, came into the room.

"What's the matter?"

"Your drunk brother just put us in it!" Tom said.

John looked at Andy.

"What did you do, brother?"

Andy looked at Tom and John with wide eyes, as if they were accusing him of something.

"Let's just eat," he said then, and rushed into the kitchen.

Outside, Clint and the lawmen came within sight of the Graham house without being approached.

"They can't be that secure," Owens said.

"Maybe they don't know what Andy just did," Mulvernon said.

"It doesn't matter," Owens said. "Let's just flank the house and get Andy out of there. Once we have him he'll give us the names of the others who were with him when he killed Tewksbury and Jacobs."

"You think he's just going to come out?" Clint asked. "Give up without a fight?"

"Actually," Owens said, "I don't care if he wants a fight. I'm tired of cleanin' up dead bodies. Maybe we need to start puttin' some into the ground ourselves."

Owens decided he'd go up to the house himself, with Clint, Mulvernon, and the two deputies flanking him, staying out of sight. Clint had to give him credit. Although he sounded like he was spoiling for a fight he was setting it up to avoid one. If the five of them had approached the house, it would have invited a fight, immediately.

They spread out and Owens walked up to the house, stopped about twenty feet from the door.

"Blevins!" he shouted. "Andy Blevins!"

*   *   *

Inside the house they heard the voice.

"This is Sheriff Commodore Perry Owens!"

Tom looked at John and said, "Goddamn your brother!"

"He's drunk," John said. "Nobody's gonna believe what he said."

"The sheriff is outside!" Tom said. "Why do you think he's here?"

"We'll just go out and talk to him," John said. "It'll be fine."

In the kitchen Andy pulled young Sam aside and said, "Somebody should put a bullet in that sheriff, kid."

"Yeah? Ya think so?"

"I think anybody who did it would be a real man," Andy said.

Sam had an old Colt strapped to his leg. He didn't keep it clean, so it was fifty-fifty that if he ever pulled the trigger it would either fire, or blow up in his hand.

"He's here to get me, Sammy, I know it," Andy said. "We're brothers, you can't let him take me."

"Then let's take him, Andy," Sam said.

"I'm drunk, kid," Andy said. "I can't shoot straight."

"Then I'll take 'im," Sam said.

"Good boy!"

John and Tom were still trying to decide what to do when Sam Blevins suddenly burst from the kitchen, pushed between them, and approached the front door, drawing his gun.

"Hey, kid!" Tom yelled, "What are ya doin'?"

John yelled, "Sammy, don't open the door!"

Sam Blevins ignored both of them. He swung the door wide open, stepped out, and started shooting at Sheriff Owens.

TWENTY-NINE

As the door opened, Owens readied himself. When the first shot came he threw himself aside and drew his gun. He fired, and his first bullet hit young Sam dead center, driving him back into the house, into John Blevins's arms.

"Ow! John, it hurts."

"What the hell were you doin'?"

"Andy said—"

"Andy!" John yelled.

Men came running from the kitchen with their guns out, proceeded to knock the windows out, and start shooting before anyone could stop them.

"Oh, shit!" Tom said.

When the first shot came, Clint and Mulvernon drew their guns. On the other side of Owens, both deputies did the same.

"Who was that?" Clint asked Mulvernon.

"I didn't see."

At that point they heard breaking glass and then the firing started from inside the house—all aimed at Owens, who started scrambling for cover.

"Goddamn it, give him some cover fire!" Clint yelled.

He and Mulvernon began to fire at the house, as did the two deputies on the other side. Owens found his way to an untethered buckboard and flipped it over for cover.

Now all five men were firing at the house.

"Jesus!" somebody in the house shouted. "How many of them are there?"

John laid Sam's body down on the floor. The boy had died in his arms. He hurried to the windows to join his family. The women were huddled in the kitchen.

Tom Graham was gone, having gone out the back door when the shooting started.

"They're on all sides," somebody yelled.

John didn't think so. He ran to the back of the house and looked out. There were no lawmen there. They were all in front. He could have fled, but he decided to go back in and stand with his relatives. Besides, someone had to pay for killing Sam, the boy.

Eventually, the men in the house started spreading out their fire, shooting at all the lawmen outside and at Clint.

Owens was pinned down behind the buckboard.

Clint and Mulvernon had found cover behind a huge pile of chopped wood.

The deputies, Pete and Jake, had each found a big enough boulder to use for cover.

They were all armed with pistols, while some of the fire from the house came from rifles. They had left their horses far from the house, to keep them safe from errant fire, and that's where their rifles were. It didn't matter, though. They were well within range for their pistols to be effective.

Clint and Mulvernon decided to time their shots so that one of them was always shooting while the other was reloading.

The deputies on the other side were too excited to plan something like that, so they kept firing and reloading together.

Clint noticed that Owens's firing was pretty measured, and that he always reloaded while others were firing. He seemed cool under pressure.

Inside the house, whatever glass was left in the windows soon became smeared with blood. The fire coming in from outside was eventually finding its mark. Blood spray covered the walls and the glass. The floor was littered with dead or injured men. The women had crawled from the kitchen to tend to the injured, and one of them had been hurt, as well.

Andy Blevins was dead, as was Sam, and so was Mose Roberts. John had been injured, and it was his decision to call a halt to the melee.

"That's it," he shouted to his remaining family members. "Stop shootin'!"

They stopped and it fell quiet.

"Sheriff!" he called out.

There was no answer right away.

"Sheriff!" he shouted again. "Sheriff. This is John Graham!"

Outside, when John Graham identified himself, Owens looked over at Mulvernon, who waved at him to go ahead and reply, since they were both sheriffs.

"Graham, this is Sheriff Commodore Perry Owens of Holbrook!"

"He loves his full name, doesn't he?" Clint said to Mulvernon.

"I guess I would, too, if I had a pretty name like that," Mulvernon said.

"We're done in here, Sheriff Owens!" John called back. "We're comin' out!"

"Toss your guns out the windows first," Owens called back. "All of the guns in the house!"

Suddenly, iron began flying out the windows—pistols and rifles, and even some knives.

Owens stood up straight, his gun in his holster. Clint and Mulvernon kept their guns out to cover Owens, just in case, and Mulvernon waved at the two deputies to come in behind the sheriff.

"All right, Graham!" Owens shouted. "You and your family come out with your hands up!"

THIRTY

They brought the Graham faction back to Holbrook. The dead were left at the undertaker's, while the living were put into cells. The injured were taken to the doctor, and then put in a cell. The women were left to go free, to make arrangements for the dead.

"So this puts an end to it," Jake said, when they were all in the sheriff's office.

"Why would it?" Mulvernon asked.

"Well . . . this is all the Grahams, isn't it?" the deputy asked.

"Not hardly," Mulvernon said. "Tom is still out there, and he started it all. And we know there's still family in the hills."

"And then there are the Tewksburys," Clint said. "Ed is still out there, and so's his family."

"But they don't have nobody to fight anymore."

"You forget," Owens said. "It's the Tewksburys who

joined up with the Dagg brothers. There are still cattle people who are not gonna stand for sheep in this valley."

"So you see," Mulvernon said, "it's not over."

"So what do we do now?" Pete Garrett asked.

"The Tewksburys are actually my concern, not yours," Mulvernon said. "Clint, me, and Jake will go back to Prescott and at least talk to some of the Tewksburys. Tell them what happened out here. Maybe that'll satisfy them for a while."

"I better talk to the judge, here," Owens said. "And the mayor. Let them know what went on today."

"They ain't gonna like it," Garrett said. "They been wantin' to avoid a bloodbath, and that's what we got, today."

"I'll just have to explain," Owens said. "Sam Blevins fired the first shot."

"Sam Blevins was fifteen years old," Garrett said.

"I know," Owens said.

"Want me to back your story?" Mulvernon asked.

"No," Owens said, "I'll go alone. They'll either believe me or they won't."

Mulvernon stood up, followed by Clint and Jake.

"We better get back to Prescott, then," he said. "The news will hit there soon enough." He shook hands with Sheriff Commodore Perry Owens. "Good luck."

Clint also shook hands, and they left.

THIRTY-ONE

Clint, Sheriff Mulvernon, and the deputy—who Clint still only knew as Jake—returned to Prescott the next morning, and put their horses up at the livery.

"I've got to see the mayor and the judge," Mulvernon said to Clint, "but we should talk after that. I'm sure you're getting anxious to be on the move."

"I am," Clint said, "but I can still put it off for a day or two. I'd like to see what effect yesterday has on the situation as a whole. Maybe Ed Tewksbury will turn himself in when he hears what happened."

"I doubt that, but we'll see," Mulvernon said. "Jake, go and let Tyler know we're back."

"Yessir."

"I'm going to my hotel," Clint said. "I'm sure they're wondering when they're going to make some money on my room."

"Don't worry about that," Mulvernon said. "The mayor insisted that your room be paid for by the town."

* * *

"When is that freeloader going to leave town?" the mayor demanded. "We've been paying for his room for weeks, now."

"And it's been worth it," Mulvernon said.

"Well . . . what do you need Adams for?" Daley asked. "Send him on his way now."

"I'm going to leave that decision to him," Mulvernon said. "He's generously given us all this time—"

"Generously?" the mayor asked. "He's been living free!"

"He's been paying for his own meals," Mulvernon said. "And, I might add, some of mine."

"Well, at least he's paying for something," the mayor said. "And his horse, right? He's paying the livery fees?"

"Well . . . I've got to get to work."

Mulvernon went out the door while Daley shouted behind him, "We're paying his livery fees, too?"

Clint stopped at the front desk of his hotel to arrange for a bath. He had just sunk into a tub of hot water—with his gun belt hanging on the back of a chair within reach—when there was a knock on the door.

"Come in!" he called, his hand touching his gun.

The door opened and a girl entered. Actually, upon second look, she was a young woman. She was dressed in trail clothes, and wore a gun on her hip. Clint kept his hand near his gun. He'd been shot at more than once by women in the past.

"Are you Clint Adams?" she asked.

"I am," he said, "and I'm taking a bath."

She closed the door and leaned against it, eyeing him with amusement.

"I can see that," she said. "My name is Janey."

"And?"

"Tewksbury," she said. "Janey Tewksbury. Ed's my pa."

"Ah," he said. "Okay, what can I do for you?"

"Well," she said, "for one you can take your hand away from your gun. I know you can shoot me down before I touch my gun. I ain't here ta hurt ya."

Warily, he drew his hand away from the gun. He still felt very vulnerable, sitting there naked in his tub of hot water.

"I was hoping to enjoy this water while it's hot, Miss Tewksbury—"

"Just call me Janey."

"Janey," he said, "is this something we can talk about later?"

"Naw," she said. "I think we should talk about it now. That water still hot?" She moved closer to take a look in the tub.

"Hey! Back up, there," he said. "Yeah, it's hot."

"I been needin' a bath for a while," she said, "and I ain't got the money. You mind?"

"Do I mind . . . what?"

"Sharin'," she said, dropping her gun belt to the floor.

"Wha—"

Stunned, he watched her shuck her shirt and trousers, getting naked in record time. Before he knew it, she was stepping into the tub with him.

THIRTY-TWO

She was not a large woman, but the room she took up in the tub was mostly by her breasts. They were large and round, with heavy undersides and large nipples. There was nothing thin about the girl. She was a tightly packed woman.

The water level rose as she settled down across from him, her legs inside his.

"You're not shy, are you?" he asked.

"Sorry," she said, "but I had a lot of boy cousins. We used to share a bathtub all the time."

"And when was the last time you did that?"

"Well, not for a long time . . . Oh, I see what you mean. Well," she said, running one of her small feet along one of his legs, "I didn't see you fighting me."

"Hey," he said, "if a sexy young woman wants to get into a bathtub with me all of her own decision, who am I to argue?"

"You think I'm sexy?"

"I think that's pretty obvious."

She looked down, saw his erection sticking out of the water.

"I seen them on my cousins," she said, "but never like that."

"Wait," he said, "don't tell me you—you're a—a—that you've never—"

"Oh, no," she said, "'course I have. Lots of times."

He wasn't sure just how much she was lying. She was at least twenty, living in a family with lots of boys—and men. She probably wasn't a virgin but she also probably didn't have much experience.

Her foot made its way to his erection and ran up and down it. She definitely *wasn't* very shy.

Sheriff Mulvernon wasn't going to go to his office, but once he was in the city hall building he changed his mind. He entered the office, found both deputies there, Tyler sitting behind his desk. When Tyler saw him he sprang to his feet.

"Stay there," Mulvernon said. "I only stopped in for a minute. I've got to go upstairs and see the mayor."

"Jake was just tellin' me what happened, Sheriff," Tyler said. "I miss everything."

"You missed a bloodbath, Tyler," Mulvernon said. "You missed having to kill people."

"I missed fighting alongside the Gunsmith, and seein' him in action."

"Yeah, well," Mulvernon said, "I would have traded places with you, believe me."

"What are we gonna do now, Sheriff?" Tyler asked.

"You stay on duty," Mulvernon said. "Jake, you're off duty. Do what you want—get cleaned up, get some rest. Be back in six hours."

"Right, boss."

"I've got to go and see our friendly mayor."

"Not so friendly," Tyler said.

"What do you mean?"

"He was in here earlier, looking for you, and he wasn't happy."

"Maybe I should just go and freshen up first—" Mulvernon started, but he stopped when the door to the office opened and the mayor filled the doorway.

"Mulvernon! When did you get back? Didn't your deputy tell you I was looking for you?"

"I just got back," Mulvernon said, "and he just told me."

"Well, come upstairs," Daley said, "we've got to talk."

Mulvernon looked at his two deputies, rolled his eyes, and followed the mayor out.

"That's hard," she said.

"Well—"

"And big," she said. "I ain't never seen one that big. I mean, that long."

"Janey—what's your game?"

She pulled her eyes away from his swollen and red cock sticking up out of the water with soap suds around it.

"My game?" she asked, looking at him.

"Are you supposed to keep me busy so some of your family members can come rushing in here and shoot me?"

"Maybe."

"What do you mean, 'maybe'?"

"I mean, maybe that's what I was supposed ta do, but now that I'm in the bathtub with you, lookin' at your talleywacker all big and hard, I forget."

She leaned forward, put her hand out, and took hold of him. He quickly checked the door and saw that she had locked it behind her. If she was supposed to keep him busy, she probably would have left the door unlocked.

She slid her hand up and down his prick, oohing and ahing at it. What the hell, he thought. He didn't invite her in, and he didn't force her into the tub with him, so why not?"

"You know," she said, "All I ever done with one of these was stuff it inside me. Then the fella sort of huffs and puffs and rolls off a me before I know what happened. That ain't the way it's supposed to be, is it?"

"No."

Sliding her hand up and down his rigid pole she looked him in the eyes.

"Can you show me what else to do with it?" she asked. "I mean, I don't wanna be no whore or nothin', but I'd sorta like ta know . . . somethin'."

"Well," he said, "I can, but—"

"Is there somethin' else you gotta do?" she asked. "Someplace else you gotta be?"

He looked at her solid breasts, totally exposed except for the fact that her nipples were in the water, felt her small hand on him.

"There might have been," he told her, "but I guess I forgot, too."

THIRTY-THREE

"This is a bloody mess," Daley said, as Mulvernon entered his office.

"Yes, for Holbrook," Mulvernon said, "not for us. For their mayor, not for you."

"I know!" Daley said, looking positively gleeful. "That's what I mean. It's a great bloody mess! How did you do it?"

"I didn't do anything," Mulvernon said, "and you sure do keep on top of things."

"I have sources in Holbrook that keep me informed," the mayor said. "For instance, your friend Owens has been sacked."

"What? Fired? Why?"

"Because of this great big bloody mess," Daley said. "Mayor Eaton, over there, thinks Owens should have found a way to stop things before they went this far."

"How the hell was he supposed to do that?" Mulvernon asked. "How could any of us do it?"

"I don't know, but you've managed to keep the lid on here," Daley said. "No bloodbaths here in Prescott, right?"

"Not yet."

Daley's face went serious.

"What do you mean, 'not yet'?"

"I mean it ain't all over yet," Mulvernon said. "There are still Tewksburys around. Ed is still out there."

"Yeah, but he hates the Grahams and they're all dead, right? Or in jail?"

"No," Mulvernon said. "Tom is still out there, and he started this all by killing the Navajo."

Daley sat down behind his desk, as if his legs had suddenly become too weak to carry his weight. He pointed a shaky finger at Mulvernon.

"You have to make sure that what happened in Apache County doesn't happen in Yavapai County, Billy," he said. "The election's next month."

"Is that all you care about?" Mulvernon asked. "Your reelection?"

"Hey," Daley said, "if I have a job, you have a job. Remember that."

Mulvernon wasn't at all sure that was true, but he kept his opinion to himself for the moment.

"What do you intend to do now?" Daley asked.

"I'm still looking for Ed Tewksbury. He committed murder and I want him in my jail."

"And Tom Graham?"

"Him, too, if I can find him."

Mulvernon walked to the door.

"Well . . . make sure you leave your deputies in town if you have to leave."

"I know my job."

"And what about Adams? Is he still helping you?"

"He is."

"Good, good," Daley said. "Forget what I said about him. You need him."

"I'll tell you who else I need."

"Who?"

"Commodore Perry Owens."

"Who?"

"The sheriff who just got fired in Holbrook," Mulvernon said. "I want to hire him as a deputy."

"We don't have the budget—"

"I need him, Mayor," Mulvernon said, "if you want me to keep the lid on."

"Oh, fine!" Daley said. "Hire him."

"I'll need to get word to him," Mulvernon said. "Is your . . . contact still in town?" He almost said "spy."

"Yes," said the mayor.

"Then send word to Owens for me," Mulvernon said. "I'd like him here by tonight."

"Yes, yes, as you wish."

"I've got work to do," Mulvernon said, and left.

THIRTY-FOUR

"So, you actually do this slowly?" Janey asked him. "I mean, you don't just rut and roll off?"

"Where's the fun in that?"

"I thought that was fun, for men," she said.

"No, it has to be fun for both the man and the woman," Clint said. "For you and me."

"I ain't never heard a man say that before."

She had his cock in both hands now, rubbing it, feeling it. She slid one hand into the water to cup his testicles, found them swollen and heavy. Then she ran her nails along the tender skin on the underside of his penis.

"Ooh," he said.

"That was good?"

"That was very good."

He reached out, took her breasts in his hands.

"I know," she said, "they're big and ugly."

"Whoever told you that?"

"Um, my father, my cousins . . . said I was too little to have teats like these. Made me look like a cow."

"Well, they're wrong," he said, holding their weight in his hands. "They're beautiful. Look, the skin is so smooth, and your nipples—"

"—they're brown. Too dark."

He thumbed them. She bit her lips and moaned.

"They're beautiful, and sensitive. Feel that?" He pinched them.

"Oh . . . yeah . . ." she breathed.

He took his hands away.

"We have to get dressed."

"What? Why?"

"The water's getting tepid," he said. "We'll go to my room . . . to bed."

"You wanna go to bed with me?"

"Very much."

"And . . . we'll go slow?"

He smiled, pulled her to him, and kissed her, a long, slow kiss. She bent her legs so that her crotch was pressed against his hardness, her breasts crushed against his chest.

"We will go very, very slow," he promised, speaking with his mouth pressed to hers.

"Well then, let's go!" she said, standing in the tub.

"But we have to get dressed," he warned her, as she stepped from the tub. "We have to go through the lobby!"

"Okay!"

They practically ran through the lobby and up the stairs to Clint's room. Once inside they hurriedly removed each other's clothes. Then Clint tried to slow things down.

"Can we go fast first?" she asked. "Then slow?"

"Whatever the lady wants."

He sat on the bed. She straddled him, slid down on him until his penis was completely inside her.

"Do you wanna put me on my back?" she asked.

"No," he said, feeling her heat around him, "this is fine."

She put her hands on his shoulders and began to ride up and down him. She was not used to doing this at her own speed. Most men would have flipped her over by now. This was a new experience.

"Ooh, Jesus," she said, riding and falling on him. The length of him that came out of her was wet, and felt cold as the air struck him, but then she came right back down on him and engulfed him in her warmth again.

"Oh, this is nice," she said, "this is very nice . . ."

"Yes, it is," he said.

He had the very male urge to turn her onto her back and fuck her hard, but he'd promised to do things at her pace. Luckily, she was quickening.

Mulvernon went back down to his office and sat behind his desk. He sent Deputy Tyler out on rounds. He didn't tell him that there was a new deputy on his way. That's because he wasn't all that sure that it would happen. He didn't trust the mayor to send his message, but he might. He was worried about his election, so he'd want Mulvernon to do his job.

He sat back and closed his eyes.

He just needed a minute.

* * *

Clint slid his hands beneath Janey's butt. She was so wet she was soaking them both.

"Okay," he said, "it's time to move."

"Fine with me," she said into his ear.

He stood, lifting her with him while keeping her impaled. He bounced her and she gasped.

"Pays to be little sometimes, huh?" she asked. "Bounce me some more!"

"The lady gets what the lady asks for," he said.

THIRTY-FIVE

Janey was an apt pupil. The first time Clint suggested she take his penis in her mouth she looked at him like he was crazy. Then she tried it, just a little bit. Then a little more.

"It's warm," she said, "and your skin is so smooth."

"Not as smooth as yours."

"That's only because I'm a girl."

The flesh of her breasts, her thighs, and her butt was as smooth as glass. It was only on her work-hardened hands that the flesh was rough and coarse—but those calluses scraping along the tender skin of his penis was . . . interesting.

But her mouth, that was avid, talented beyond belief. She did things with her tongue . . . things she shouldn't have known how to do. They either came naturally to her, or she was lying to him. . . .

* * *

Janey was a quick study, and pretty soon—well, hours, actually—he was returning the favor. He slid down between her thighs and the first time he touched her with his tongue she started as if she'd been hit by lightning. Moments later she sighed contentedly as he worked on her with his tongue, his lips, and even his teeth.

"Oh my God," she said. "I never thought . . . never knew . . ."

She was gasping, then, unable to speak as her orgasm overcame her.

"Wow," she said, moments later. "Was that . . ."

"A big one," he said.

"Wow."

They lay on their backs side by side.

"Are there other things you can show me?" she asked.

"There are," he said, "but it'll have to wait."

"For what?"

"For me to get some rest."

She started to argue, then stopped, thought, and said, "Yeah, I'm pretty tired, too."

"Then I suggest we get some sleep," he said.

She snuggled up to him, put her head on his chest, and said, "Okay by me."

In moments, they were asleep.

Mulvernon woke behind his desk with a start, and almost fell out of his chair. The door had opened and Jake had walked in.

"Sorry, Sheriff."

Mulvernon wiped his eyes.

"What time is it?"

"Time for my shift."

Mulvernon's stomach growled.

"And time for me to get something to eat," he said.
"And maybe a bath."

He got up and headed for the door.

"You can sit behind my desk, if you want," he said, as
he went out the door.

Clint felt her take her head off his chest and slide from
the bed. She could have been doing it carefully so as not
to wake him, or . . .

He grabbed his gun from the holster hanging on the
bedpost, turned, and pointed. Still naked, she had her
gun pointed at him.

"Stand off," he said. "You want to put it down, or
should we shoot it out?"

She bit her lip.

"You'll lose," he told her.

"I . . . I can't . . ."

"You can't put it down?"

She licked her lips. A tear formed in her eye.

"No, I mean, I can't kill you."

She lowered the gun, but still held it in both hands.

"Who sent you?"

"My father."

"Ed?"

She nodded.

"Listen, Janey—is it Janey?"

"Yeah, I'm still Janey."

"Why don't you put the gun down? We'll get dressed
and go get something to eat, and talk."

"You ain't gonna kill me?" she asked.

"No," he said, "I'm not going to kill you."

"Why not?"

"Maybe I'm just too hungry to do it now," he said, getting off the bed. "Or maybe it has something to do with the fact that we're both naked."

He picked up her clothes and tossed them to her.

THIRTY-SIX

Clint took Janey to the same restaurant Mulvernon had taken him to several times for chewy steak. Janey ordered a steak, while he ordered beef stew in which the beef was not as tough.

"Where is your father?" Clint asked.

"In the hills."

"Does he know that most of the Graham and Blevins families are dead? Killed in a shoot-out with the law?"

She stared at him.

"I don't know," she said.

"Did you know it?"

"No."

"Then maybe he doesn't, either."

"He just sent me here to town to . . . to kill you."

"Why did he think you would do it?" Clint asked.

"I—I always do what my father tells me to."

"So, you're not as . . . inexperienced as you made yourself out to be."

She looked down.

"No." She looked at him. "But that doesn't change the fact that you are not like any man I've ever met before."

"I suppose I should say thank you."

"No," she said, "I should say that. I didn't think I'd have trouble killin' you, because I've always thought men were the same—like the men in my family. Like my . . . father."

Clint didn't ask, but he was fairly sure her own sexual experience with men came with members of her family—including her father. It was no wonder she'd be ready and willing to kill a man.

"But you're not like them," she said. "And maybe there are even more like you, and less like them."

"Jesus," he said, "I hope so."

The waitress came with their food just as Sheriff Mulvernon walked through the front door. Clint waved at him.

"Why don't you join us?" he said to the lawman. "I've got someone I want you to meet."

Mulvernon looked at Janey, who didn't look happy.

"You're gonna turn me in?"

"Not exactly," he said. "Just eat. That's what the sheriff came in to do. Right, Sheriff?"

"Right."

Mulvernon told the waitress to bring him a steak dinner.

"Are you sure?" Clint asked.

"Old habits," Mulvernon said. "Who's the young lady?"

"Somebody you're going to be interested to meet," Clint said. "Janey Tewksbury."

"Tewksbury?" He looked at her.

"My daddy's Ed Tewksbury," she said, "and I don't much care if you kill him."

"Do you know where he is?"

"Only that he's in the hills," she said.

"That's no more than we know now," Mulvernon said.

"Yeah," she said, around a big hunk of steak, "but I know where he's gonna be tomorrow."

Both men looked at her.

"Where?"

"I'm supposed to meet him, to let him know I did . . . what I was supposed to do."

"Which was what, exactly?" Mulvernon asked.

"Kill me," Clint said.

"What?"

"I'll explain later. Where are you meeting him, Janey?"

"About ten miles out of town, in a shallow wash not far from our house."

"Will he be alone?" Mulvernon asked.

"I don't know."

"Why would he bring anyone if he was just meeting her?" Clint asked.

"Because he doesn't know if she actually killed you or not," Mulvernon said. "Maybe you caught her, and you were making her bring you to him."

"Which is what we'll be doing," Clint said.

"Right," Mulvernon said. "So if I was him I'd have some men with me."

"Then we should bring some men with us," Clint said. "Your deputies, Tyler and Jake."

"And Owens."

"Owens?"

Mulvernon nodded.

"He got fired," he said, "and I'm hiring him on as a deputy—if he'll take the job."

"When will he be here?"

"Soon, I hope. Tonight."

"Good."

"Who's Owens?" Janey asked.

"Finish your steak," Clint said.

THIRTY-SEVEN

Janey wanted to go back to Clint's room with him. She asked him after Mulvernon left them alone at the table.

"No."

"Why?" she asked. "Is it because I was going to kill you?"

"No, that's not it."

"Then what?"

"You lied to me."

"A woman has never lied to you?"

"Many have," he said. "None of them got into my bed again."

"Then what am I supposed to do until tomorrow?"

"What do you mean?"

"I mean where am I supposed to sleep?"

"Well . . . get a room."

"I don't have any money."

"Your father sent you here with no money?"

"Well, I figured I'd end up sleepin' in your room."

"After you killed me?"

"Or before."

"Sorry," he said.

"Then where—"

"We'll find somewhere," he said. "Come on."

Mulvernon looked up when Commodore Perry Owens walked into his office. He was surprised. Apparently Mayor Daley had delivered his message.

"Heard you needed a deputy."

"Glad to see you. Sorry about you being fired."

"It was time," Owens said with a shrug.

"Have a seat."

Owens sat down. He was unshaven and looked as if he had ridden hard.

Mulvernon opened his desk drawer, took out a deputy's badge, and dropped it on top of the desk.

"Yours if you want it."

Owens took off his hat and scratched his head.

"You still going after Graham and Tewksbury?" he asked.

"Yes."

Owens sat forward and picked up the badge.

"I'll wear it until we finish this thing," Owens said. "After that, no promises."

"That's all right with me," Mulvernon said. "Who's taking your place in Holbrook?"

"My deputy."

"Is he . . . capable?"

"Are yours?"

"Not very."

"There ya go."

"So we don't need to bring him in on this?"

"I don't think so."

Owens picked up the badge and pinned it on.

"I'm gonna get settled," he said. "Get a room and a bath. When are we goin' out?"

"In the morning," Mulvernon said. "We know where Ed Tewksbury is going to be tomorrow."

"How'd you come by that little bit of information?" Owens asked.

"His daughter."

"Can she be trusted?"

"I doubt it," Mulvernon said. "She actually came here to kill Clint."

"Didn't get it done?"

"No."

Owens nodded, stood up.

"If you want to eat I can tell you where to go," Muvlernon said.

"Tell me," Owens said, "and then I'll know where not to go."

Clint found a rooming house for Janey. He handed her some money.

"You ain't comin' in?"

"No. The woman who runs the place probably wouldn't like that."

"You know her?"

"No, but ladies who run rooming houses are usually fussy about that. You go ahead, get a room and I'll see you here in the morning."

She grabbed his arm as he turned to leave.

"What am I supposed to do until then?"

"Try getting some rest."

"We could get some rest together," she said, then added, "or not."

"I'll see you in the morning, Janey."

She removed her hand. He watched her enter the house, then turned to walk back to his hotel.

THIRTY-EIGHT

Clint met with Sheriff Mulvernon, his two deputies, and his new deputy, Commodore Perry Owens, at the sheriff's office in the morning.

"We ready to do this?" Clint asked.

"What time did Janey say she was supposed to meet her father?"

"She was told to be there around midday. He'd either be waiting, or he'd come later."

"If he comes at all," Owens said.

Clint looked at Owens, saw the badge on his shirt.

"Welcome to Prescott, Deputy," he said. "Nice to have you."

"Happy to be here," Owens said. "You're the one I'm dependin' on to tell me where to eat."

"The hotel's got a good dining room," Clint said. "Stay away from anyplace the sheriff eats."

"I figured out that much already," Owens said.

"That's enough chitchat," Mulvernon said. "Let's go and pick up your girl."

Mulvernon headed for the door, followed by his deputies.

Clint looked at Owens and said, "She's not my girl."

"Chitchat?" Owens said.

They collected their horses from the livery, and asked the man there which horse belonged to Janey. They had to describe her, but the man finally pointed out a small mare. They saddled her and took her over to the rooming house.

When Janey came out of the house she had an odd look on her face.

"What is it?" Clint asked.

"The woman who lives here," she said. "She . . . talked to me last night, until late."

"So?"

"She's very . . . nice."

"And you're not used to that?"

"The women in my family are hard," she said.

"Made that way by the men they live with, no doubt," Clint said.

"She wants me to eat breakfast before we leave."

"We don't have—" Mulvernon started, but Janey cut him off.

"She says you can all eat," Janey said. "She's making flapjacks, bacon, and biscuits."

Clint looked at Mulvernon.

"We can spare half an hour, can't we?"

Mulvernon looked around him. All the men were waiting for his answer.

"Okay," he said, "let's eat."

Bellies full, they mounted their horses an hour later, with still plenty of time to get to the meeting place by midday.

"Take the lead, Janey," Clint said.

"And you should know," Owens said, "if you're leadin' us into a trap you get my first bullet."

Janey looked at Clint. He knew what she was thinking. *This man is not like you, more like my father.*

"He's just doing his job," he said to her. She gigged her horse and trotted ahead.

"Clint, you ride up front with Janey. We'll watch our back trail."

"At some point you should send someone ahead of us," Clint said. "I'll find out from her where we're going."

"Okay."

Clint nodded, and rode ahead to join Janey.

Clint had met many liars in his life, and the thing that struck him about all of them was how many times they did it. Sometimes they were incapable of telling the truth. Even when they were caught in a lie they'd just tell another one.

He had no idea if Janey was telling the truth now—if she was even capable of telling the truth. She'd been under her father's domination for her whole life. What happened in the hours ahead was going to depend on whether or not she had the strength to break free—the strength, and the desire.

"Have you ever tried to leave before, Janey?" he asked.

"Leave?" she asked. "You mean, leave home?"

"Yes."

"I never had any reason to."

"And now you do?"

"Yes."

"Why?"

"I told you, I never met anybody like you before," she said.

"You had sex with me and everything changed?"

"It wasn't the sex," she said. "It was you. The kind of man you are. And then Mrs. Brewster, the kind of woman she is."

"So it's all different now."

"Yes," she said, "it's all different now."

Nothing ever sounded more like a lie to him.

THIRTY-NINE

"Okay," Janey said a couple of hours later. "It's about a mile ahead. If we—"

"Wait a minute," Clint said. He turned in his saddle, called Mulvernon and Owens to ride up alongside them.

"Janey says we're about a mile away."

"Straight ahead," she added.

"I'll send Tyler ahead—"

"I don't think we need to do that," Clint said.

"Why not?"

Clint looked at Janey.

"Because I think she's lying to us."

"What?" she said, contriving to look hurt.

"I think Tewksbury's there with a bunch of men, or else he'd just send some men to meet us."

"How do you want to play it, then?" Mulvernon asked. He did not question how Clint knew Janey was lying.

"I think we should split into two groups, come at them from both sides."

"Okay," Mulvernon said. "I'll take my boys around to the east, Owens can go with you to the west. What about the girl?"

"I'll take her," Clint said.

"Remember what I said, missy," Owens told her.

"Are you gonna let him threaten me?" she demanded of Clint.

"If this isn't a trap, Janey," Clint said, "I'll make him apologize. If it is . . . my bullet will be the second one you feel."

"She won't feel it," Owens said. "She'll already be dead from mine."

Janey did not look happy.

"How are we going to know when we're all there?" Mulvernon asked.

"That'll be easy," Clint said. "It'll be when the shooting starts."

"Right," Mulvernon said. "Good luck."

"You, too."

Clint turned and waved at the two deputies, who still didn't know what was going on, but waved back.

"Let's go," Owens said.

"Wait." He took out a bandana from his saddlebags, reached over, and tied it around Janey's mouth. She went to take it off but he grabbed her arm.

"Leave it!"

She scowled at him, but left it in place.

Next, Clint plucked her gun from her holster, and stuck it in his belt.

"Now let's go," he said to Owens, who was laughing.

* * *

Clint, Owens, and Janey circled wide to the west and then started to come in on what they hoped was Ed Tewksbury's position. If Janey was lying, she could have been lying about everything. But Tewksbury was a hunted man, and his concern would be to get the hunters off his trail.

An ambush was the perfect way to do that.

"Hold up," Clint said, raising his hand.

Owens reined in, looked over at Janey right away to be sure she was behaving. Her eyes were humping around in her head.

"She's nervous," Owens said. "I think we should keep her in front of us."

"Sounds good to me," Clint said.

She shook her head frantically.

"Why not?" Clint asked.

She said something that was muffled by the gag on her mouth.

"Oh, sorry," Clint said. "I'll take it off, but if you yell . . ."

She shook her head frantically again, indicating she wouldn't.

Clint pulled the gag down from her mouth.

"Don't send me in there, they'll kill me."

"Who will kill you?" Clint asked.

"My goddamned trigger-happy cousins," she said. "They'll start shootin' as soon as they see somebody."

"And what about your father?" Owens asked. "Is Ed there?"

"No," she said, glumly, "he won't be there."

Clint and Owens exchanged a glance.

"How many?" Owens asked.

"Six, I think," she said, "maybe more if they picked up some other men."

"How do we play this?" Owens asked.

Clint was about to answer when they heard shots coming from close ahead of them.

"I think somebody's already made that decision for us," Clint said. "Come on!"

FORTY

Clint and Owens reached the action when it was in full swing. Owens had hold of the reins of Janey's horse, and she was fighting him. He finally had to release her so she wouldn't get him killed.

Clint and Owens drew their guns. They both decided to go with their pistols, not rifles, because they were going to get as close as they could.

Ahead of them Mulvernon, Jake, and Tyler, had been pinned down by more than six men, who were firing from the cover of a formation of rocks. Clint could see that this place had been carefully picked. The Tewksbury men had good cover, except they didn't know that Clint and Owens were coming from the other direction.

Clint fired first, followed by Owens. Both their shots were well placed—two men were spun around by the hot lead and dumped onto the ground.

The Tewksbury men suddenly realized they were in a cross fire. Some of them turned to face Clint and Owens, while the others continued to trade shots with Mulvernon and his deputies.

Clint figured they were facing ten men—eight, since he and Owens had each taken care of one. The men in the rocks panicked when they saw that Clint and Owens were not dismounting and taking cover. They rode their horses right at the men, unnerving them.

On the other side, Mulvernon saw what Clint and Owens were doing. He stood up and started running at the Tewksbury men, his deputies following.

Now the Tewksbury men felt the pinch, with all the lawmen rushing at them. Their nerve broke and suddenly they scattered, trying to get away. They tossed shots behind them, but they were hurried and haphazard. They were just trying to get away. Clint, Owens, Mulvernon, and the deputies were methodical and, in minutes, they had shot down all of the Tewksbury men.

It became eerily silent suddenly. Gun smoke floated away as the lawmen approached the fallen men to check them.

"Anybody alive?" Mulvernon asked. "Find somebody who's still alive so we can question them."

They walked among the fallen, but found none of them still breathing.

"Anybody hurt?" Clint asked.

"Here!" Tyler said. "Jake took some lead in his shoulder."

They turned, saw Tyler holding Jake up. The other deputy was bleeding from a shoulder wound.

"Okay," Mulvernon said, helping Tyler with Jake. "Let's get him down and check him out."

"Anybody else?" Clint asked.

"I'm fine," Owens said.

"Where's Janey?"

Clint looked around, and spotted her lying on the ground. Her horse had apparently run off. Maybe the animal had dumped her in a panic.

He trotted over to her, but as he approached he could see a splash of red across her chest. When he reached her and looked down he saw the blood coming from her mouth. There were bubbles, which meant she was still alive.

He leaned over her.

"Janey?"

Her eyes fluttered open and she looked up at him. His head cast a shadow across her face, keeping the sun out of her eyes.

"D-did ya get 'em?"

"Yeah, we got 'em."

"All?"

"Yes."

"Good," she said. "B-bastards." She sprayed blood when she said it.

"Janey," he said, "where's your dad?"

She coughed, and a gob of blood came from her mouth and rolled down over her chin.

"I'm gonna die, ain't I?"

"Yes."

"B-bastards," she said again. "One of them idiots shot me."

"Yes, they did." He didn't know if it was one of the Tewksbury men or Mulvernon and his deputies who had shot her, but he let her believe what she wanted.

"Where is he, Janey?" Clint asked. "He's no father to you, never has been. Let us get him, too."

"Y-young," she said.

"What?"

"Y-young," she said.

"I don't know what you mea—"

But she was dead.

He stood up, walked over to where Mulvernon was working on Jake's shoulder while Tyler and Owens looked on.

"How is she?" Owens asked.

"Dead."

"Get anythin' from, her?"

"Not much," Clint said. "In fact, nothing. All she said was 'young.'"

"Young?" Owens asked.

"Yes, that's what it sounded like."

Owens looked at Mulvernon, who had finished packing Jake's wound.

"Young, Arizona," Mulvernon said. "A town not far from here."

"I didn't know there was a town called Young," Clint said. "I asked her where her father was and she said Young."

"Another trap?" Owens asked.

"I don't think so," Clint said. "She was pretty mad, figures somebody from her own family killed her."

"Well, Jake needs a doctor and they've got one in Young," Mulvernon said.

"Is that closer than going back to Prescott?" Clint asked.

"A lot closer," Mulvernon said.

"Okay," Clint said, "then Young it is. Perry and I will go and round up the horses."

"I'll come, too," Tyler said.

"Let's go," Clint said.

FORTY-ONE

Young, Arizona, was smaller than Holbrook. It did, however, have a doctor and a telegraph office. As the five men rode in they attracted plenty of attention—especially since one of them had blood all down the front of his shirt.

One man got curious enough to approach the five men, who reined in rather than ride them down.

"Um, you need a doctor?" the man asked.

"We do," Mulvernon said. "I'm Sheriff Mulvernon from Prescott, these are my deputies."

"Doc's office is down the street. Above the hardware store, and across the street from the sheriff's office."

"And is there a sheriff in the sheriff's office?" Mulvernon asked.

"Nope," the man said. "Hasn't been for a few weeks, since he was killed."

Mulvernon turned and said to his men, "Let's get

Jake to the doc's. We can find out what happened to the sheriff later."

"And if Tewksbury is around," Owens said.

"Later," Mulvernon said. To the young man he said, "Thanks."

They rode down the street until they came to the hardware store. On the corner they saw a shingle that read DOCTOR JOHN MILBURN, M.D. Mulvernon and Tyler got Jake off his horse and up the stairs to the doctor's office. Over his shoulder Mulvernon called out, "Why don't you two check out the sheriff's office."

"Okay," Clint called back.

He and Owens crossed the street and entered the sheriff's office. There was three weeks' worth of dust on everything, some spiderwebs.

Owens walked to the desk while Clint approached the gun rack.

"These guns need cleaning," he said.

Owens ran his finger along the top of the desk.

"Did that fella say weeks?" he asked. "It looks like nobody's been here for months."

He opened the top drawer, saw a sheriff's badge along with some deputy stars.

"All the tin stars are here."

"So no deputies, either."

"Maybe that's why Tewksbury came here," Owens said. "He knows there's no law."

"So he's either here, or he's coming here," Clint said. "We've got to find out which."

Owens looked at some Wanted posters, went through

some more drawers. Clint went back into the cell block. All he found was more dust.

When Clint came out Owens said, "There's nothin' here. Let's go see how Jake's doin'."

Clint nodded. They left the office and crossed the street to the doctor's office.

Doc Milburn was in his sixties, with a great shock of white hair and bushy white eyebrows. He had blue eyes that sparkled and looked like they belonged to a much younger man.

He came out into his waiting room, found Clint and Owens waiting with Mulvernon and Tyler.

"He'll be okay," he said, wiping his hands on a towel. "I got the bullet out. It was real close to the bone, though, so he's gonna be sore for quite a while."

"Can he ride?" Mulvernon asked.

"I wouldn't advise it," the doc said. "I bandaged him, but riding might open the wound again. I'd put him in the hotel and let him rest for a few days."

"Okay, Doc," Mulvernon said. "We'll do that."

"He's unconscious now," the doctor said. "Come and get him in a couple of hours."

"Okay, Doc. Thanks."

"You can settle your bill then, as well."

Mulvernon nodded. He left with Clint, Owens, and Tyler.

"What'd you find in the sheriff's office?" he asked when they reached the street.

"Dust," Clint said.

"And more dust," Owens said.

"Okay," Mulvernon said, "let's split up and see if we can spot Tewksbury."

"He might not be in town yet," Owens pointed out.

"Right," Mulvernon said, "and if Janey lied, even on her deathbed, he may not be coming here at all. We'll just have to wait and see."

"Split into twos?" Clint asked. "Or go our own ways?"

Mulvernon thought a moment.

"Tewksbury might not be alone," he said, finally. "I'll take Tyler, and you two stay together. Let's just each take one side of the street."

"Okay," Clint said.

"If you spot him, just wave, don't yell," Mulvernon said. "We don't want to alert him that we're here."

"Right," Clint said.

"Let's do it," Mulvernon said.

FORTY-TWO

It didn't take Clint and Owens long to find something, but it wasn't what they were looking for. It wasn't a big town. There were two saloons, and they were across from each other. Clint and Owens stopped in front of one of the saloons, peered in a window so as not to be seen from inside.

"Well, I'll be," Owens said.

"He's in there?"

"No, he's not," Owens said, "but I see John and Tom Graham, and Charley Blevins."

"What's John Graham doing here?" Clint asked. "I thought he was in jail in Holbrook?"

"He was," Owens said, "but before I left, the judge let him out."

"Why?"

"Graham claimed the shooting was started by Sam Blevins," Owens said. "He claimed he was just trying to protect the women. I suppose the judge bought it."

"That doesn't make sense," Clint said. "With all the dead—"

"I don't know what to tell you, Clint," Owens said. "There he is."

"Okay," Clint said. "Where?"

"See there? In the corner? There are five men sitting there, but three of them are Grahams and Charley Blevins."

Clint looked around the room, saw that it was about half full.

"How many of these other men are with them?" he wondered.

"I can't tell," Owens said. "I don't see any more Grahams or Blevins, but their families are so big."

"Okay," Clint said, "why don't we go across the street to get Mulvernon and Tyler, rather than wave from here. We'll have to see how he wants to play it.'

"Why don't I stay here?" Owens said. "Keep an eye on them."

"Okay," Clint said. "I'll be right across the street. I think I saw them go into the saloon."

Clint crossed over while Owens stared at the window, watching the three seated men to see if they interacted with anyone else in the room.

Clint found Mulvernon and Tyler in the saloon across the street.

"We found them," he said.

"Tewksbury?"

"Tom Graham," Clint said. "Along with John Graham and Charley Blevins."

"Graham?" Tyler asked. "Not Tewksbury?"

"Maybe that's why Tewksbury was coming here," Mulvernon said. "He knew this was where Graham was."

"Well, it doesn't matter," Mulvernon said. "Tewksbury or Graham, they're both fugitives." He looked around. "Where's Owens?"

"He stayed across the street to keep an eye on Graham," Clint said. "He has four men sitting with him, but we don't know how many more in the saloon might be with him."

"Owens is staying outside, right?" Mulvernon asked. "I mean, he won't go in, right?"

"Why would he go in there on his own?" Clint asked. "That would be crazy . . . right?"

They ran outside, looked across, and saw that there was no one in front of the saloon.

FORTY-THREE

Owens approached the table of five men and said, "Tom Graham?"

Graham looked up, saw the badge on Owens's chest.

"Deputy Owens, Prescott," Owens said. "You're under arrest."

"Owens," John Graham said. "Prescott? What happened to sheriff of Holbrook?"

"I didn't want to be sheriff of a town that would let you out, John. You're under arrest, too."

"What about us?" Charley Blevins asked, indicating himself and the other two men at the table.

"Yeah, you, too."

Owens kept his eyes on all five, but his main concern was Tom Graham. The others would move when he did.

"You made a big mistake comin' in here, Sheriff," Tom Graham said.

"Is that so?"

"It is."

"It's Deputy, not Sheriff."

"It don't matter what it is," Tom said. "You're dead either way."

Owens drew his gun quickly—so quickly that two of the men at the table jerked back, startled.

"Let's go."

"Your mistake," Tom said, "was assumin' that we were here alone. See, we got other friends in this saloon."

"That's okay," Owens said, "I got other friends across the street."

"Yeah, but that's where your friends are, and mine are in this saloon—behind you."

Owens heard the hammers being thumbed back on several pistols behind him.

He cocked his own weapon.

"You're gonna go first, Tom," he said, "way before I do."

"I don't much care, Owens," Tom said. "Most of my family is dead. I was just waitin' here because I heard Ed Tewksbury was comin' to town. I tell you what? Why don't you let me take care of him, and then you can take me in."

"All of you?"

"No," Tom said, "I'm just talkin' for me. These other fellas will have to make their own deal."

"I don't make deals with the law," Charley Blevins said.

"Well, there ya go, Sheriff," Tom said. "No deals."

"That suits me, Tom," Owens said. "Tell your boys to start shootin'."

* * *

Clint, Mulvernon, and Tyler got to the front of the saloon and stopped. They peered in the window, saw Owens standing in front of the five men with his gun out. Behind him were three other men with their guns out.

"I count eight," Clint said.

"Tyler," Mulvernon said, "count to five and throw something through this window."

"Like what?"

"Something that will break it and attract attention," the sheriff said. "And then start shooting."

"Yessir."

Clint and Mulvernon moved to either side of the batwing doors. Tyler looked around, saw a wooden chair leaning against the wall. He picked it up. It felt kind of flimsy, but he thought it would do the trick—if he threw it hard enough.

He threw it, hoping it wouldn't bounce off.

FORTY-FOUR

Clint and Mulvernon burst into the saloon just as the chair went through the window. Shards of glass flew all over as everyone in the place turned to look at the window—except Commodore Perry Owens.

"What the—" Tom Graham said.

He saw the chair come through, saw the man outside the window, and then saw the two men coming through the batwing doors with their guns drawn. He looked at Owens, saw the man looking right at him.

"Take him! Take him!" he yelled at the men at his table.

Tom Graham upended the table.

Clint saw the three men who had been holding guns to Owens's back quickly turn to look at him and Mulvernon. Their eyes went wide and they started to turn. He heard someone shout, "Take him! Take him!" He didn't know who it was, but he and Mulvernon had their hands full with these three.

From the window, Tyler started shooting at the three men. As Mulvernon fired his gun, Clint decided Owens was going to need his help. He threw himself to the side and hit the floor, but held on to his gun. He saw Tom Graham flip his table and all five men started to get up, drawing their guns.

Commodore Perry Owens's gun was already out, but Clint knew he was still going to need help. He started firing from his position, prone on the floor.

Owens started pulling his trigger as soon as he saw the look in Tom Graham's eyes. His first bullet hit Graham in the chest as the man flipped the table. After that, Owens had to step back to avoid the table, but he kept firing.

All of the patrons of the saloon who weren't firing were hitting the floor. The bartender ducked down behind the bar. He had a scattergun back there, but he didn't want any part of the action.

John Graham and Charley Blevins scrambled for their guns as the table flipped. The two men with them did the same, but they were too slow. Owens shot both of them before they could get their guns out.

Graham and Blevins had a bead on Owens, but at that moment Clint's shots pinned them to the wall. Owens saw the bullets hit home, but fired his own gun at them anyway. They slid down to the floor, leaving a bloody trail on the wall behind them.

Owens turned, saw Clint on the floor, and waved.

* * *

Tyler came climbing through the window as the shooting stopped. The three men he and Mulvernon had shot were on the floor. The saloon got quiet and people began to lift their heads.

Clint got to his feet, walked over to where Owens was checking the bodies. They were all dead, except for Tom Graham, and he soon would be.

Owens and Clint both leaned over him.

"It was Ed," he said, as blood bubbled from his mouth, "Ed Tewksbury killed—killed my brother—"

"Tell us something we don't know," Clint said, as the man died.

"Dead?" Mulvernon asked from across the room.

"Yep," Clint said. "All of them."

"Here, too," Mulvernon said.

Clint and Owens walked back to where Mulvernon and Tyler were standing. People had gotten back to their feet, were either sitting at their tables, bellying back up to the bar, or leaving.

"Looks like we're done," Tyler said.

"All except Ed Tewksbury," Mulvernon said, "and whatever distant relatives he can dig up."

"I think," Clint said, "I'm going to leave it to you and your deputies to pick up Jake."

"Clearing out?"

Clint nodded.

"I'll ride back to Prescott with you, but then I'm done. Time for me to get moving."

"Well," Mulvernon said, "we appreciate your help, Clint." He looked at Owens. "Looks like this town might need a sheriff."

Owens grinned and said, "That's exactly what I was thinkin'."

Just outside of town Ed Tewksbury reined his horse in and turned. He had just been riding into town when he heard the shooting. Whatever was going on, he didn't want any part of it.

He turned and rode away.

AUTHOR'S NOTE

The basic premise of this story is true. The Pleasant Valley War was fought between the Tewksbury and Graham factions (the Grahams including the Blevins brothers). Ed Tewksbury was eventually arrested by Sheriff Mulvernon. He was tried twice. The first time the trial ended in a hung jury. The second time he got off on a technicality. Tewksbury finally died of natural causes in Globe, Arizona, in April 1904.

Watch for

THE LADY DOCTOR'S ALIBI

339th novel in the exciting GUNSMITH series
from Jove

Coming in March!

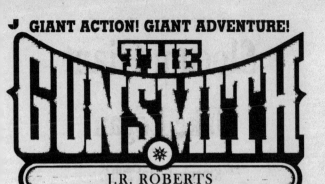

GIANT ACTION! GIANT ADVENTURE!

THE GUNSMITH

J.R. ROBERTS

penguin.com/actionwesterns

M455AS0509

DON'T MISS A YEAR OF

Slocum Giant
by
Jake Logan

penguin.com/actionwesterns